The Rift

THE RIFT

Kim Antieau

Green Snake

PUBLISHING

The Rift
by Kim Antieau

Copyright © 2012 by Kim Antieau

ISBN-13: 978-1-949644-19-7

All Rights Reserved.

Cover photo by Kim Antieau.
Book design by Mario Milosevic.

Special thanks to Nancy Milosevic and Ruth Ford Biersdorf.

No part of this book may be reproduced
without written permission of the author.

Electronic editions of this book are
available at most e-book stores.

Published by Green Snake Publishing
www.greensnakepublishing.com

www.kimantieau.com

for all the edge dwellers
and their kin

FIRST

Sonora Desert, January,
Full moon, Blue moon, Lunar Eclipse

Maggie lived in the desert on the edge of the city limits of Tucson, Arizona, in a casita near a wash that filled with water once a year and threatened to overflow and flood Maggie's house and her shop. Every year Maggie stood on the lip of the wash as the water roared through and asked very politely if the New River would please stay away from her house. She threw flower petals into the water to seal the deal.

In ten years, the wash had not breached its banks.

Maggie was generally a contented person. She enjoyed working with people and trying to find the right desert plant that would help them heal. She liked going out into the desert and talking with plants, wildcrafting for tinctures, or plucking blossoms (with permission) to make flower essences.

She lived outside the mainstream of American life. She didn't watch television, wasn't on any social networking site, got most of her clothes from Goodwill, and had no idea about the private lives of anyone famous.

Maggie didn't make a living talking with plants or helping people heal. She didn't make a living howling with the coyotes at sunset or following the path of a bobcat at dawn. She didn't make a living whispering to the wind and discussing the weather with the crows. But she did create her life in this manner.

For a steady income, Maggie edited technical manuals from home. She didn't particularly like this work—wasn't overly fond of computers—but she was good at taking nonsense sentences and turning them into sensible sentences. Her boss said she was the best translator of geek in the business. Maggie didn't tell him she was good at many languages: geek, crow, cactus, road runner.

She was not always good at translating human.

She wasn't awkward with people. She had social graces. She could nod and say, "Uh-huh," with the best of them. With people she knew, however, Maggie spoke her mind and her truth. Her friends valued that about her—even though she sometimes frightened them.

Especially men. At least men who wanted to have sex with her. Maggie had never batted her eyelashes or pretended she was more interested in a man's opinion than she was in her own. In fact, she couldn't believe women still did that. Her friends introduced her to their male friends sometimes at dinner parties or celebrations. At the end of the night, the man usually left with a younger woman.

 KIM ANTIEAU

"He doesn't know what he's missing," whichever friend it was would say.

"Yes, I am amazing," Maggie would agree.

Maggie did not spend a lot of time thinking about men or sex. She did wish she was sexually attracted to women. Once she mentioned this to Joanna, her partner in Desert Bloomers, and Joanna said, "Women are a pain in the ass, too. They always want to know what you're thinking. You're supposed to be sensitive to their needs, and I'm just not that sensitive."

Sometimes Maggie did get lonely for her own kind, but she wasn't quite sure who her own kind was. She had friends of all persuasions: flora and human and other fauna, elementals and Invisibles.

When Maggie woke up that Full Moon Blue Moon morning, she felt off-kilter. First thing she did was get out of bed and shiver as her feet hit the cold tile floor. Then she padded to the front door of her casita to let out her dog Irving. When her hand touched the door handle, she remembered Irving was long dead. Three months now.

Old habits died hard.

Yet she had heard him barking.

Must have been a dream.

She opened the door and stepped outside. The pink dirt was cold against her bare soles. She turned to the east where the sun was coming up over the Rincon Mountains. She raised her arms and whispered a prayer to the wind and to the east. Some mornings she offered cornmeal or a song. This morning she whispered,

"Thank you for inspiration."

She turned to the south.

"Thank you for the fire of creativity."

To the west.

"Thank you for the ocean that courses through my veins."

To the north.

"Thank you for the earth, that place where I stand my ground, and the place of rebirth."

She breathed deeply.

She still felt muddled.

A breeze wound its way through the mesquite and cholla and around the paloverde, and Maggie heard, "This is the day everything changes."

Maggie knew she should thank the Wind for the warning. Or the prediction. She often told her clients that one must learn to go with the flow: Change was inevitable.

But this morning when she heard, "This is the day everything changes," Maggie thought, "Oh crap."

Too much had changed this year. For one thing, Irving had died. Her father had had major heart surgery. One of her sisters had become holy. Maggie's landlord had upped her rent when she couldn't come up with a down payment to buy the place. And Joanna told her last week that Alexandria had a job offer in Seattle, so they might be moving. Which would mean they'd no longer be partners in Desert Bloomers.

More change was coming?

Maggie started to go back into the casita when she noticed a coyote walking by in the wash. He stopped and looked at her. She loved coyotes the way people loved beautiful sunsets. Some coyotes were more spectacular than others. Some were just ho-hum. Not that Maggie really ever thought of coyotes as ho-hum. But every once in a while one crossed her path that made the hair on the back of her neck stand up. And this coyote was one of those. She'd seen him before, many times. He had a scar on his right haunch. She called him Old Brandy. Seemed like he was always on the prowl. Maggie got the sense he was lookin' for the ladies.

Now he stared at her, his tongue hanging out. Looked like he was grinning.

"I'm not your kind," Maggie said. "So move along."

The coyote continued to stare.

"Yeah, you've heard me howling, but I wasn't calling to you."

He closed his mouth. Now he looked a little dangerous. Maggie growled.

The coyote put his nose in the air for an instant, glanced at her, and then kept walking—bouncing down the wash as though he was walking on his tiptoes.

"I don't know why you don't like that coyote," Joanna said as she came across the wash toward Maggie. "I think he has a crush on you."

"That would be flattering," Maggie said. "Kind of like having one of those old drunks at the East Side Bar and Grill have a crush on me."

Joanna laughed. "I swear I've seen coyote tails on some of those men."

"Old Brandy is probably one of them," Maggie said. "And I don't dislike him. I'm just wary. You're up bright and early. What's going on?"

"Just had a feeling it's going to be a day," Joanna said. "I've got two appointments but—"

Maggie nodded. "Yep. Something's up."

"John and Nina thought they saw lights coming over

the Rincons last night," Joanna said. "Swear it was a whole group of UFOs. But then they're always seeing that kind of thing."

Maggie shrugged. "Hey, I talk to plants. Most people think that's weird."

"But do you think the plants came here from outer space?"

"Maybe originally. I've never asked."

Joanna grinned. "Go eat. I'll catch you later. I may need your help when Alan Josephson comes in. He picks up little pockets of energy like he was flypaper. Might need help cleaning him off."

Maggie nodded. She went back into the house, sat on her living room floor, and meditated. Her mind kept drifting. She wished she could remember her dream about Irving.

When she finished meditating, Maggie made oatmeal. She took the bowl with her to the back porch and looked out into the desert as she ate. A shiny green hummingbird flew around her for a moment. Maggie held out the bowl of oatmeal to the bird. "You're welcome to it," she said, "but it's got nothing on nectar." The hummingbird flew away west, in the direction of a tall saguaro with two limbs raised up in a kind of cacti yoga pose. The day smelled very slightly of creosote.

Maggie closed her eyes. "May it be good, may it be good, may it be good," she whispered.

She heard someone banging on her front door. She got up, carried the bowl into the kitchen, put it on the counter, and then went to the door. She wasn't sure she wanted to open it, but she did.

"Margarita! Rita! We need your help!"

It was her neighbor Ricardo. She had known him ten

years and had not been able to convince him that her name was Maggie, not Margarita. Not Rita.

She glanced at Ricardo. He didn't appear to be injured.

"What is it?" She came outside. Ricardo's old white pickup stood in her driveway with his teenaged daughter Alicia kneeling in the back of it.

Maggie hurried over to the pickup.

Sprawled on the truck bed was a man. He reeked of alcohol so much that Maggie had to lean back away from the truck.

"Whoa!" she said. "Is he hurt?"

"*Sí*," Ricardo said. "His heart is broken. And he can't stop drinking. We've tried. All of his friends have tried."

The man's jeans were ripped and caked with mud. His T-shirt was dusty, and the shirt over the T-shirt was so dirty Maggie couldn't tell what color it was. His dark brown hair was greasy and his face was covered in stubble.

"I think he tried to drown himself in the wash," Alicia said.

"In the wash?" Maggie said. "There's no water in the wash."

"*Exactamente,*" Ricardo said. "He's loco. He went out for a walk about an hour ago. I went looking for him with the truck and found him stumbling out of the wash and into the road."

"Can you do anything?" Alicia asked. "Mom's about had it with him. But he needs somebody's help."

Maggie looked at Alicia. She still believed in the natural goodness of everyone, believed everyone could be saved.

She'd grow out of that soon enough.

Ouch, Maggie thought. When had she gotten so cynical? Maybe she had picked up some negative energy herself.

"Are you sure he doesn't need a doctor?" Maggie asked. "Could he have taken some pills?"

Ricardo shook his head. "No, he's just your ordinary drunk."

"Alicia, go into the shop and get Joanna," Maggie said. "Then open the bunkhouse door. We'll put him in there."

Alicia hopped out of the truck and ran toward the barn.

Ricardo pulled down the tailgate. Maggie jumped up into the truck bed.

"What's his name?" Maggie asked.

"Jack," Ricardo said.

"Jack!" Maggie said loudly. "Jack, you need to wake up."

The man moaned.

Maggie felt his pulses. They were strong.

"Jack, you need to get up."

The man moaned again.

Maggie nodded to Ricardo. He got into the truck bed. Together they lifted Jack into a sitting position.

Jack mumbled something.

"We're going to take you someplace where you'll feel better," Maggie said.

Joanna and Alicia walked over to the end of the truck bed and each grabbed one of Jack's legs. They pulled while Ricardo and Maggie pushed until Jack was sitting on the edge of the tailgate.

"Should we carry him?" Joanna asked.

"I think you should move out of the way," Maggie said.

Everyone moved away from Jack.

He promptly threw up.

"Better here than in the bunkhouse," Joanna said.

"Yep," Maggie said. "Get it all out of your system now."

Maggie put Jack's left arm around her shoulders and her right arm around his waist. Ricardo did the same on Jack's right side. They half-dragged, half-walked Jack into the bunkhouse—the guest room that doubled as an extra treatment room—and laid him on the bed.

"Let's get these clothes off," Maggie said. "He stinks like a sewer. No telling what's on these things."

"I will do it," Ricardo said.

"It'll be easier if we all do it," Maggie said.

Ricardo shook his head. He motioned to Alicia to leave. She rolled her eyes but left the bunkhouse.

"I don't think there's anything underneath," Ricardo said.

Joanna smiled. "Ricardo, we've seen naked men before."

He looked at her.

"Yes, even me," Joanna said. "I used to dabble in men a bit, before I saw the light."

"Me, I haven't seen a man in a long time," Maggie said. "I think I've forgotten what they look like. Let's get his clothes off for a better look."

Ricardo stared at them.

"I thought this was an emergency," Maggie said.

"The sooner you go, the sooner I take off his clothes," Ricardo said.

"Oh good grief," Joanna said. "All right. There are

gowns and pajamas and stuff in there." She pointed to a dresser across the room.

The three women waited outside while Ricardo helped Jack get undressed. Maggie could hear Ricardo arguing with the incoherent Jack. "But I gotta piss, man."

Maggie looked at Joanna. "Please let him make it to the toilet."

A few minutes later, a pale Ricardo emerged carrying Jack's clothes.

"I'll take them home to wash and bring them back later," he said. "Thank you for your help. He's a good man, really." He started to walk away with Alicia. Then he stopped and turned around. "I got his clothes off, but I didn't get any clothes on."

Joanna and Maggie went into the bunkhouse. Jack still lay on his back. Now he was snoring, his mouth open. Ricardo had pulled the sheet up over Jack's naked body.

Joanna went to his feet, Maggie to his head. Maggie closed her eyes. She imagined roots growing out of the soles of her feet into the earth. Imagined the main root going down deep while smaller roots went horizontal into the earth until they found other roots to twine around. Then she imagined the energy of the earth coming up the roots and filling her body until the energy spilled out of the crown of her head. She put her hands on Jack's head.

She felt or heard a kind of thump, as though the earth had shifted deep beneath them. She looked at Joanna; Joanna shrugged.

Maggie pressed her hands lightly on either side of Jack's head. She imagined healing light flowing into the top of her head, down her shoulders and arms and out

   KIM ANTIEAU

the palm of her hands. Her hands tingled. Jack stopped snoring.

Maggie felt slightly dizzy. That happened sometimes when she worked on someone. It passed. The room felt like it was filled with creatures, most of them desert creatures.

"He feels overshadowed," Joanna said.

Maggie nodded. "But I'm not sure by what."

"The alcohol? The plant spirits of the alcohol? Agave?"

No images came to Maggie. She felt slightly seasick, the way she did sometimes when she walked the wash when it hadn't rained in a very long time.

Usually a plant spirit would offer to help during a healing. Or Maggie would get an image of what the client needed.

Not this time.

"My hands are warm," Maggie said. "So he is drawing the healing energy into his body."

"I'd like to stay and help," Joanna said, "but I've got a client in about five minutes. I've got pulses in his feet. Plus, I see he's got a little something going on beneath the sheets."

Maggie looked down at Jack. She laughed softly.

"They can't help it," Joanna said. She slowly took her hands off of Jack's feet. Then she left, closing the door behind her.

Maggie looked down at Jack again. Just then his eyes snapped open. His eyes were yellow. Maggie blinked. No, they were blue. Bright blue. Jack smiled sleepily.

"Hello, *bruja*," he said. "Are you the one I've been looking for?"

"I doubt it," Maggie said.

"I think you are," he said. "What's under the sheets doesn't lie."

"Charming," Maggie said.

Jack closed his eyes. "Your friend started it. I was just trying to hold up my end of the conversation. So to speak."

"Your job right now is to get this alcohol out of your system," she said.

"After all the trouble I went through to get into my system? Seems like a waste of a good time."

He began breathing deeply again. Maggie moved her hands from his head and down to his chest. His skin was cold. She felt grief. Intense grief. He put his left hand over her left hand. His fingers were clammy. She moved her right hand down to his belly. Warm. She could feel his stomach gurgling under her hand.

"It's all right," she whispered. "It's all right. This is the place and the time that heals all wounds."

"Even yours?" he whispered.

Ah, so he was awake.

"Shhhh," she said.

"No," he said. "I have to know if you're the one."

Maggie shook her head. Of course she wasn't the one, whatever that meant.

"You'll know the answer to that when you wake up," she said.

"I'll hold you to that," he said. "I will. I'll hold you real close."

 KIM ANTIEAU

NEXT

NEXT

Maggie sat on a stool at the end of the bed with her hands on Jack's feet. She loved when she had her hands on someone while doing a healing. It felt like love streamed through her and into the other person. Didn't matter who they were. She didn't have to do anything but be open and let it flow.

Of course learning to be open and learning to let it flow took a few years of practice. Especially being open. Sometimes it was easier just to shut down. When she was with people in "ordinary time" rather than in "healing time," as she called it, she could feel herself folding in, like a flower when the sun went down. Even when she wasn't folded in, she was definitely surrounded by prickly barbs: a desert flower. She was particularly suited for the desert.

Lots of people hated the desert. They didn't see the beauty in it the way they saw beauty in a wooded glen, an old growth forest, or an ocean beach. She liked the desert because it was not soft and cuddly. You had to stay alert. You had to realize that death was right around the corner. Life, too. After a while, the desert and its creatures became like old friends who turned out to be wizards and witches with all sorts of magic to share.

At least that was how Maggie saw it.

In any case, she liked being with people best during "the healing time." Then all of her energy was focused on . . . detecting energy. When she listened to someone tell her what was bothering them, she heard more than their words. She heard what was underneath, sensed what was underneath. She wasn't exactly sure how she did it. More years of practice. She wasn't anything special. She wasn't anyone special. She had just practiced. She had learned the art of interpretation.

Sometimes all of life felt like one big interpretation, didn't it?

Like now, she believed she was helping this man Jack heal. That was her truth. Could there be another truth or was truth only one thing?

The facts were the facts. But truth?

She shook her head.

She was still feeling muddled this morning. She wondered when the eclipse had started. Supposedly eclipses created openings in the space-time continuum. Or it was a time when the veil between worlds became thinner. Or whatever a person experienced during the two week period between the lunar eclipse and the solar eclipse would be magnified or multiplied during the coming year.

Maggie wasn't sure if any of that was true. She just knew she felt a little bit of a quiver in the world during the day of the full moon. And on the night of a full moon, sometimes everything seemed to shimmer. Especially out here in the desert.

Maggie finally lifted her hands from Jack's feet.

She went into the bathroom and washed up. She heard Jack's voice from the other room say softly, "You don't have to stay with me."

Maggie came out of the bathroom drying her hands on a towel. Jack was sitting up, slightly, leaning on his elbows.

"I don't want you to pass out, vomit, and aspirate." she said.

"Not a pretty picture." He closed his eyes. "I didn't have that much to drink," he said. "Just a couple shots of tequila."

"You seemed pretty hammered for two drinks."

He shrugged. "Coyotes can't drink. Haven't you ever heard that?"

"Coyote?" Maggie moved closer to Jack.

"Yeah, I'm Coyote Jack. Pleased to make your acquaintance." He lifted the sheet and looked under it.

"Damn," he said. "You got me naked awful fast." He looked up and grinned at her.

"Ricardo did that. He couldn't get you to put any clean clothes on. You want to try now?"

"Only if you'll stay and watch."

Maggie sighed. "Is that your version of charm? Cuz I gotta tell you it's completely lost on me. For one thing, you smell like shit. For another thing, you're dirty. And you're drunk. What woman, man, or beast could resist that?"

She thought he flinched a little. Maybe just a twitch

in his left cheek. She pressed her lips together. Hadn't Ricardo said he had a broken heart? She should take better care.

She went to the dresser, opened it, and pulled out a dusty-blue pair of scrubs. She put them on the bed.

"Do you want to sleep now or take a shower?" she asked.

"I think I'll just rest here for a minute if you don't mind," he said. He leaned back and closed his eyes.

Nothing like kicking a man when he's down, Maggie thought.

"What'd you say?" Jack asked. "Drinkin' fries my hearing sometimes."

"Nothing," Maggie said. She hadn't said anything out loud, had she?

Joanna opened the door and peeked in. "How's he doing?"

"He's doing just fine with two beautiful women looking after him," Jack murmured. "Lilith and Eve. Aphrodite and Venus. Gaia and Earth Mother."

Maggie turned to look at him.

"More like Kali and Hecate," she said.

"I was going to say them next," Jack said.

Joanna motioned to Maggie, and they went outside. Maggie pulled the door closed behind her.

"Hey, Alan Josephson called," Joanna said. "He can't get through. They're not letting anyone come down Speedway or Broadway past Tanque Verde. There's a giant sinkhole or a crevasse, maybe caused by an earthquake. Something happened and the ground shifted or fell and there's a huge break that goes across Speedway and down Freeman and across Broadway."

"And you can't drive across it?" Maggie asked.

"Apparently not. It's too wide, and they don't know exactly what happened or if it'll happen again."

Maggie and Joanna looked at one another. Both knew this meant everything east of the crack in the earth was essentially boxed in. Speedway and Broadway both dead-ended at the park leading up to the Rincon Mountains. All side roads led to Speedway or Broadway.

"Maybe we better find out what's going on," Maggie said.

She quietly opened the door to the bunkhouse and looked inside. Jack appeared to be asleep. She closed the door again. She and Joanna walked away from the barn and toward the wash. A crow dropped down from the tall paloverde over the wash and headed straight for them. Maggie ducked as it flew over.

"Geez," she said as they turned to follow the crow's flight west. "I've never seen that happen."

"Almost like it suddenly decided it was a swallow," Joanna said.

They were about to step into the wash when Joanna grabbed Maggie's arm. They both stood frozen for a moment as they stared at the sand.

Dozens of snakes were sidewinding down the wash, swimming in the sea of sand.

Dozens of *rattlesnakes*.

The women took a couple of steps away from the wash.

Maggie had lived in this desert for ten years and had never seen a rattlesnake in the winter. She could count on one hand how many she'd seen in the summer.

Maggie did not dislike snakes. She liked the idea of them slip-sliding through life with their bellies up close and personal to Mother Earth. And because snakes were vilified by so many patriarchal religions, Maggie felt a particular kinship with them. However, she knew enough to be wary of real-life rattlesnakes who were not symbolic of anything and who could strike out if given provocation. Like hunger. Or fear.

Or downright craziness. This looked like someone had dropped a ball of twined snakes into the wash and now each snake was peeling away from the ball and heading south down the wash.

In the next instant, Maggie heard the familiar low grunting squeal of javelinas. She looked around until she saw a herd of them running through the wash from the north, headed right toward the rattlesnakes who were continuing south down the wash.

Javelinas had notoriously bad eyesight and could easily hurt a person in their rush to get . . . anywhere. Maggie and Joanna sprinted across the drive to Maggie's front step and watched from there as the javelinas ran and squealed. It was all so noisy and chaotic, like a carnival ride gone bad. Maggie heard the distinctive rattle of a snake poised to strike. That couldn't be good.

And then the cacophony continued downstream, as it were, until the sounds faded away and the day once again pulsed with desert silence.

"What was that?" Joanna asked.

"Cats and dogs living together, I guess," Maggie said. "Must have something to do with the earthquake, or whatever it was. Come on."

They looked both ways—just in case something else was coming their way—and then they ran across the wash. They hurried down the long driveway and walked the dirt road until they got to Speedway, the paved road that went from the east end of Tucson all the way to the west end—mile after mile after mile. During heavy traffic it felt like the longest city street in the world. Of course out here in horse country, away from town, they hardly ever encountered heavy traffic.

And now there was no traffic at all.

Maggie and Joanna turned left on Speedway and headed toward the flashing lights in the near distance. Maggie heard coyotes howling somewhere in the desert.

"By the way, Jack's full name is Coyote Jack," Maggie said.

"Huh," Joanna said. "Maybe he's actually Old Brandy, come to show you a good time."

"Yeah, so far it's been a great time," Maggie said. "I think I was a little nasty to him. Didn't mean to be. All his good ol' boy flirting just got on my nerves. I'm too old for that shit."

"You were always too old for that shit," Joanna said. "The guy's stewing in his own juices. He's probably just looking for some dignity."

They saw Nina and John walking down their drive toward Speedway and stopped and waited for them. John's T-shirt had an alien head on it with the words, "What's probed in Tucson stays in Tucson," written below it. Maggie chuckled.

"You think your aliens did this?" Joanna asked as they continued down Speedway.

"They're not *our* aliens," Nina said. She shrugged. "Or maybe they are. Maybe we were sent here to spy on you all."

Ricardo pulled up beside them in his white pickup. He slapped his door. "Get in."

Maggie waved to Lisa, Ricardo's wife, who sat in the

front seat. The four of them got in the back with Alicia. The truck bed no longer smelled like liquor and vomit.

Ricardo drove a short distance, then stopped. They all got out of the truck and walked slowly to the crack in the road.

Only it was more than a crack. It was a kind of chasm. The pavement disappeared into blackness. Maggie looked down and couldn't see the bottom. It was startling that the earth could move that way.

The chasm looked to be about ten feet wide.

On the other side of the rift were police cruisers, fire trucks, an ambulance, hazmat truck, and several black sedans, all with their flashing lights on. Maggie's stomach flip-flopped a bit.

"Was anyone hurt?" Maggie asked.

On the other side of the chasm, a tall red-headed man with a clipboard looked over at her.

"I'm Jeff Shaw," he said, "head of Emergency Management. We're assessing the situation, but as far as we can tell, no one was hurt."

"What caused it?" Maggie asked.

"We don't know yet," he said.

"So when will the road be fixed?" John asked.

"We won't know any of that for a while," Shaw said, "since we don't know what happened."

"How far does it go?" Joanna asked.

"Quite a ways north and south," he said.

"So we're stuck here," John said.

"Keep tuned to the public access channel and we'll let you know what's happening," he said. "And keep children and pets away from the edge."

"Yeah, like that's gonna be our biggest problem," Lisa murmured.

  KIM ANTIEAU

"Hey, have you had any reports of animals acting funny?" Joanna asked the Emergency Management guy.

"What have you encountered?" Shaw asked.

"We just saw a bunch of rattlesnakes all tangled together in the wash," Joanna said. "Then they untangled and slid away followed by a pack of javelinas."

"I don't think javelinas run in packs," John said.

Joanna glanced over at him. "Okay, followed by a gang of javelinas."

"Gangster javelinas?" Alicia said. "Coolness."

The man with the clipboard was busy writing.

Maggie frowned. "Probably has nothing to do with anything," she said.

Joanna looked at her. Maggie tried to smile nonchalantly.

"We'll check it out," Shaw said. Then he turned away from them.

"What was that all about?" Joanna whispered. "Why didn't you want me to tell him anything?"

"I don't know," Maggie said. "Something about this seems strange."

Maggie squinted and tried to see who was inside the black sedans. A man and woman in uniform stood next to the ambulance. The firefighters stood next to their truck. But the people in the sedans were hidden behind tinted glass.

"It's such a cliché," John said as he came to stand next to Maggie.

"What?"

"The men in black in the black cars," he said. "Looking for aliens."

"They do look like g-men," Nina said. "Maybe we shouldn't have reported the sighting last night."

"You called someone?" Maggie asked.

"We always try to," Nina said, "you know, to document it. There's so many around here. And last night there were colored lights and a kind of triangle shape. But I didn't expect this."

"You didn't expect what?" Lisa asked. "You think the government caused this rift? The airport flight path goes right over the Rincon Mountains. All you're ever seeing are some goddamn passenger jets, not alien ships."

Maggie glanced at Lisa and then at Nina and John. They looked at one another and shrugged. What was up with Lisa?

"Yeah, that's probably all it was," Nina said.

"Nothing we can do from here," Ricardo said.

"Good thing it's Sunday," Nina said, "or everyone would be on the other side, at work."

Maggie smiled. Nina could always find the bright side of almost anything.

"That means no school tomorrow," Alicia said. "I don't know if I'm happy or sad about that."

They turned around and began walking back to the truck.

"How is Jack doing?" Ricardo asked.

"Who cares about him?" Lisa asked. "I swear, Ricardo, you and Alicia will pick up any stray and bring him home. Now you've left him on Maggie's doorstep. Where's he gonna go now? Eh? He could be some psycho serial killer for all you know."

"For all I know you are a psycho serial killer," Ricardo said. He winked at Maggie, and she smiled.

"I thought Jack was a friend of yours," Maggie said.

"He is," Ricardo said. "A true blood brother friend."

"Hah!" Lisa said. "He's been helping Ricardo on the job. That's all he knows about him."

"He has shared with me his heart," Ricardo said. "I know he is a good man. Trust me. I knew you were a good woman when everyone around me said, oh no, that woman, she is loco."

Lisa rolled her eyes. "Watch out, old man. I can kill you in your sleep any time I like."

Ricardo patted his belly. "But then you would miss all this lovin'!"

"Dad," Alicia said. "You and Mom. We're out in public and you're talking about murder and sex."

"You want we talk about the weather?" Ricardo said. He shrugged. "It's sunny and warm. There you go."

"To answer your question, Jack will be fine as far as I can tell," Maggie said. "He just needs to sleep it off."

Ricardo shook his head. "He needs more than that, Maggie, he needs more than that."

Ricardo and Lisa got in the truck and the rest of them piled into the back. Ricardo turned the truck around and drove away from the rift and dropped Joanna and Maggie off at the end of Maggie's drive. The women walked toward the house.

"My other client lives on the other side of the rift, too," Joanna said, "so I guess I'm free for the day. I could make some more tinctures, but I'm hoping Alexandria decided to stay home instead of going hiking with Jeri. Glad we live on this side. You don't think this has anything to do with what Nina and John saw last night, do you?"

"No," Maggie said. "More likely it's a shift in the space-time continuum."

Joanna laughed. Then she stopped. "You are kidding, aren't you?"

Maggie smiled. "We'll see, my pretty one. We'll see."

"I hate it when you do that witch from *Wizard of Oz,*" Joanna said. "It's a little freaky how dead on you are."

Maggie shrugged. "But I liked her. She wasn't wicked. She was empowered."

Joanna laughed. "I'm getting out of here before I get tangled up with a bunch of rattlesnakes. I'll call you later."

Maggie watched as Joanna drove away. She wondered how long it would be before everyone wished they were on the other side of the rift. She heard the hiss of a snake and looked around. It sounded like it was coming from all directions. Then she realized it was just the sound of the wind through the mesquite tree behind her. She slapped off the dust on her jeans and headed for the barn. Time to check on her patient.

NEXT

Maggie looked in on Jack. He was sleeping. The bunk-house now stank of alcohol. He reached for her hand, in his sleep, as she checked his pulses. Reached for her as she left. She wondered who had broken his heart. She didn't know men like him could get their hearts broken.

Men like him?

What a judgmental little twit she was today.

She left Jack and went back outside. She had an uncomfortable urge to follow the path the rattlesnakes had taken. Uncomfortable because she did not want to be confronted by a bevy of rattlesnakes. Even if they had something to tell her, she wasn't sure she'd be able to hear it through the deafening roar of her terrified heartbeat. She was not a fearful person by nature, but she was cautious.

One stayed alive in the wild by knowing when to be cautious and when to leap into the fray—and in a sense that was being cautious, too, because you judged when it was safe to leap.

She did not know what was up with all this chatter going on in her head today.

"You can keep gabbing," she said to herself, "but I've got things to do."

She stepped into the wash and started walking south. Eventually Fifth Street cut the wash off on the south end, just as Speedway cut it off in the north. She looked down at her feet but saw no traces of the sidewinders. The javelina hooves must have trampled all traces of the snakes.

Maggie walked slowly and listened intently. She heard a wren go "chuk, chuk, chuk." And she heard her own feet crunching over the dirt. But that was it. She saw no hide, hair, or scale of any rattlesnakes. Not that rattlesnakes had scales. Fish had scales.

Maggie kept alert as she walked through the wash. She wondered where all the snakes had come from and where they had gone. She had lived in the desert long enough to know that the wild creatures who wanted to stay hidden would stay hidden.

She followed the curves of the dry stream bed until she came out onto Fifth Street. She looked both ways down the dirt road. No traffic. She headed west, up over the rise, toward Freeman. She passed by Joan Doud's house. Her property ended where Maggie's started, and when Maggie walked through the wash, she passed through Joan's property, as well as McKean's and Dimmitt's. But they had always viewed the wash as a common area, an informal easement everyone abided by. Maggie hoped the snakes had not gone up into Joan's property. Her horses were as skittish as she was. Or

   KIM ANTIEAU

maybe *because* she was. Maggie waved at the house as she went by even though she didn't see anyone.

She looked ahead and then stopped. From here, she could see the chasm more clearly. It was a black slash that went north and south for as far as Maggie could see. And standing on the edge just before the pavement broke, on this side of it, was a row of crows, looking across to the other side like spectators at a sideshow. Two police cruisers were parked diagonally on the other side with their lights flashing.

Maggie heard the click and slide of a rifle behind her. She turned around. Bill Boyle was walking down Fifth Street, aiming his rifle at something beyond her.

"Bill," Maggie said. "What are you doing?"

He came over and stood beside her. "They're nothing but pests."

"Crows? What'd they ever do to you?"

"They've just been sitting there staring since it happened. It's creepy."

"Did you see it happen?" Maggie asked. "The rift, I mean."

"I felt something," he said. "Neighborhood dogs started barking, so I came out and then I saw it. Saw the birds come. Earlier there were wrens and swallows. Quail. All on the ground. And none of them flew over the rift."

"Maybe they're running from the law," Maggie said.

Bill looked at her. She smiled. "Ah, come on, Bill. Now you won't be bothered with all of those tourists at the park. You'll have some peace and quiet."

"There's already a bunch there," he said. "When they get done hiking and can't get home, what's going to happen? Is the government going to force us to house them? I ain't gonna let that happen."

"Aren't you jumping the gun, so to speak?" Maggie asked. "Earthquakes happen all the time. They'll fix the road. Life will return to normal. Nobody's going to force us to do anything. Might be fun having some new blood around here. Looks like the old blood is getting a little paranoid. Tilly know you're out here threatening to kill off the area wildlife?"

"She's still sleeping," he said. "She had a bad night."

"I'm sorry to hear that," Maggie said. "Let me know if I can do anything."

"I don't think your plant spirit thingies are going to help her now."

Bill held the gun up to his cheek as though he was going to fire it.

"Those police officers might shoot back," Maggie said, "after your bullets go right through one of those skinny ass crows."

Bill let the barrel of the gun point up, and he pulled the trigger.

The sound made Maggie jump and her ears ring. The crows scattered and flew in all the directions—except west over the rift. Policemen got out of each cruiser and kept their doors between them and Bill as they aimed guns at him.

Bill chuckled. "What are they going to do?"

"The crows might file a complaint."

Bill turned around and headed back down the road toward his house. "If this isn't over soon, it ain't gonna be pretty," he said.

"Bill, you always brighten my day," Maggie called

after him. "Never fails." He kept walking. "Call me if Tilly needs me." She watched him until he disappeared into the desert. She shook her head. "Psycho." She turned toward the rift. The police watched her. She waved. Then she walked back to the wash and headed home.

Maggie heated up black bean soup for lunch and sat out back while she ate it. A bright red cardinal was perched on the pencil cholla at the edge of her walled garden. She had not seen a cardinal in this area in months, maybe even years. Whatever had happened was certainly stirring up the animals. The cardinal stared at her, and she at him. She said, "Hello." He kept staring. "I intend no harm," she said. "What's up with you?" Either the bird was behaving strangely or she was.

She closed her eyes, imagined growing roots into the ground, imagined the green power of the Earth flowing back up her roots and into her body. She breathed deeply and tried to tune into whatever was happening in her desert.

Usually she could sense something: She couldn't quite put into words what it was. A kind of rhythm to a place. A feeling. She could tell if a cougar was near because the area around her felt tense: Sometimes it was too quiet, sometimes the birds were alarming one after another so Maggie knew where the cougar was walking. Sometimes it felt as though the desert was holding its breath. Waiting for something. A storm. Sunset. She always sensed *something* underneath what she could perceive with her five senses.

Today she felt no underneath.

Maybe that was because it was all above now?

When she finished her lunch, she got a bowl of the soup and took it into the bunkhouse. Jack was asleep.

"Jack?" she said.

He opened his eyes and looked at her.

"That smells good," he said. He sat up a little straighter than he had earlier. "Never again. I hate that feeling afterward. The whole world feels just a little too shaky."

Maggie handed him the bowl of soup.

"Thank you, ma'am."

She crossed the room to the small kitchen and got him a glass of water. She put the glass on the nightstand next to the bed.

"This is a cozy little deal here," he said. "Any chance I could stay a spell?"

"You might have to," she said. "There's been an earthquake or something and the roads out of here are impassable, as least for now. They'll probably have it fixed tomorrow or the next day."

"An earthquake?"

"The ground separated and there's about a ten foot rift in the ground," Maggie said. "I assume it was an earthquake."

Jack held his spoon between his mouth and the bowl and got very still, as though he was listening.

"Something is different," he said. "It's quiet. A little too quiet." He grinned. "Naw, I'm just foolin' with you. I can't tell if anything is different. I can tell I stink. And I ain't got no clothes. I had a few at Ricardo's."

"I'm sure he'll bring them over later," she said. "He was going to wash yours."

"Lisa gets a hold of them, she'll rip them up for sure," he said. "Not sure why she took such a dislike to me."

"She doesn't like coyotes," Maggie said. "Or canines of any kind."

"You sayin' I'm a dog?"

"You said your name is Coyote Jack," Maggie said. "I'm just keeping up my end of the conversation."

"What is this place?" he asked. "Can I do some work for you to pay for my room and your trouble?"

"This place is where I live," Maggie said. "My friend Joanna and I have a small operation called Desert Bloomers. I make plant spirit essences, mostly from blossoms."

"I never heard of anything like that," Jack said. "Do you have to kill the plant spirit to get its essence?"

Maggie smiled and shook her head. Was he making fun of her?

"No, it's a kind of vibrational medicine. There's more to us than our physical body and the vibrations of these plants can help all our energy bodies to line up and work together so that we're happier and healthier."

"But how do you get the essence of the plant?"

Maggie looked at him. She couldn't imagine he was actually interested. She answered him anyway.

"The sunlight, water, and blossoms work together in a kind of alchemical process to hold the vibrations of the plant in the water. The plant is not harmed. And I always ask permission. I often don't even use the actual physical essences, though. Mostly the plant spirit comes and helps."

"Did any come to help me today?" he asked.

Maggie shook her head. "No. I guess you didn't need them."

"I just needed you?" He held out the empty bowl to

her. "That was delicious. I feel like I could eat a horse. You got any of those around here?"

Maggie took the bowl from him.

"Yep, got one in my freezer."

Jack laughed. "I love a woman with a sense of humor."

"You have no idea what that means to me," she said.

"I think I do," he said.

Maggie smiled.

"What's your name?" he asked.

"I'm sorry," she said. "I'm Maggie."

"Maggie what?"

"Maggie Cactus."

"Really?"

"It is now," she said.

"What'd you make it up right here and now so you wouldn't have to tell me your real name?"

"What makes you think that's not my real name?" she asked. "Isn't your real name Coyote Jack?"

"I don't think so," he said. "So if I go out there in the world and tell Ricardo I know Maggie Cactus, he'll know who I'm talking about?"

"First off, you can't say you know me just because I told you my name," Maggie said. "And Ricardo has never called me by anything other than Rita, or Margarita."

"Oh, so you are Rita," he said. "I've heard about you. You're the bruja. I have been looking for you."

"That's what you said. I've been here all along. What did you want with me?"

"I want a brew that could keep me from falling in love," he said. "I've got such a soft heart when it comes to the ladies."

"I don't think you need any kind of brew right now," Maggie said. "Besides, I don't make love potions."

"You've never made one for yourself?"

"Years ago when I was younger and stupid," Maggie said.

"Did you ask for someone like me?" he said. "I'm available."

"I think you need to get some rest," she said.

"Wait," he said. "I want to know the rest of the story. Did the love potion work? Who did you ask for?"

"I asked for a companion who would love me no matter what, who would love me for exactly who I am."

"And?"

"And Irving came into my life and he was a great companion for fifteen years."

"Irving? What kind of name is Irving? Where is he now? Was he a good companion?"

"The best," Maggie said. "Always had a wet nose for me."

"He's a dog?"

"He was. He died three months ago."

"Dogs are canines. So are coyotes. Maybe I'm his replacement." He touched his palm to his nose. "Dry." He licked his palm and then pressed it against the tip of his nose. "It's wet now."

Maggie shook her head. This was one of the strangest conversations she had ever had with anyone. And she wasn't quite sure why she was having it.

"You can stay here until the rift is fixed," Maggie said, "but then you need to move on. This is definitely women's country."

"Except for Irving," he said.

"Except for Irving."

Someone knocked on the door. Maggie opened it. Ricardo stood outside holding a pile of clothes.

"Come on in, Ricardo," Jack said. "Maggie Cactus and I were just having a conversation about the relationship between man and woman vis-à-vis the canine world." Jack slowly got out of bed. He was no longer naked. At some point he must have put on the scrubs.

Ricardo frowned and stepped inside the room. "Maggie Cactus?" he said.

Maggie laughed. "That's the first time I've ever heard you call me Maggie."

"I didn't call you that," he said. "I was just saying the name. I don't know who Maggie Cactus is."

"Hah!" Jack said. "I knew she was not telling me the whole truth." He took the clothes from Ricardo and set them on the bed. "I thought I had these all folded. Pack rat get to them?"

"Only if you're calling my wife a pack rat," Ricardo said, "which I know you wouldn't do."

"I hear ya, buddy," Jack said, "loud and clear. Now if you all will excuse me, I'm gonna take a shower."

Jack picked up a shirt and a pair of jeans from the clothes pile and went into the bathroom and closed the door. A moment later, they heard the water come on in the shower.

"Does your internet work?" Ricardo asked.

"I haven't tried it this morning," she said. "Why?"

"Ours is out," he said. "Nina and John's, too."

"I can check in the shop," she said.

They left the bunkhouse and went next door into Desert Bloomers. The one room shop was about the same size as the bunkhouse but its walls were lined with shelves, and the shelves were filled with different sizes of colored bottles, some empty, others filled with tinctures or flower essences. To one side of the room was a treatment table. Drums, rocks, rattles, and crystals had homes on the shelves, too. On the counter was a computer.

Maggie touched the computer and the screen came on. She refreshed the screen. The little ball spun for a while and then a message came on the screen that said she was not connected to the internet.

"Guess we don't have it here either," Maggie said. "Did you call?"

"It was busy," Ricardo said. "Something does not seem right about all of this."

"I agree."

"They're not telling us what's going on," he said. "Maybe gas is leaking or something. Maybe there's been a horrible toxic spill. That's what people are wondering."

Just then the phone rang. They both jumped. Maggie picked it up.

"Hello?"

She heard an automated woman's voice saying, "This is a recording from the Tucson Office of Emergency Management. If you are receiving this message it means you live east of the geological incident which occurred at 9:08 a.m. this morning. Everything is being done to correct the situation at this time. We assure you that you are safe and your needs will be met. You can call the number at the end of this message if you need food or any medicine."

Maggie reached for a pencil and a piece of paper.

"We repeat, there is nothing to fear. Everything is being done to correct the situation. Please do not try to cross the rift on your own. We will have road repair crews out as soon as possible. We also need to know exactly how many people are staying in your home and who they are so we can better assess the needs of the people in the affected communities. Please call—" Maggie wrote down the number. "Your calls are important to us and they will be answered in the order in which they were received. If you would like to hear this message again, please press one."

Maggie hung up the phone.

"It was a message from the city telling us we have nothing to worry about," Maggie said. "Kind of reminds me of when someone says they're not lying and you know they are."

Ricardo nodded.

"They still didn't say what caused the rift," Maggie said.

"Did they say anything about the internet?" Ricardo said.

"No, but I bet you got the same message at home."

Ricardo took out his cell phone and pressed a button. Nothing happened. He tried again. "It says I have no service here."

"You still have a land line though, right?" she asked.

He nodded. "I better get home. Why don't you come over later for dinner and we can talk about this. Jack too."

"Will Lisa be all right with that?"

He shrugged. "If she gets mad at me, I'll just blame you."

Maggie laughed. "Ah, where to put the blame. The secret of a happy marriage."

"Or at least a long one."

NEXT

Before the dust had settled after Ricardo drove away, Maggie saw Joanna coming up the drive riding Boxer, her black (with three white socks) mare.

Maggie walked toward her. Joanna reined in Boxer, then dismounted. Maggie touched Boxer's downy nose.

"Alexandria isn't home," Joanna said. "She and Jeri went out hiking." Joanna led Boxer to the corral and dropped his reins over the fence. Then Maggie and Joanna walked toward the shop. "I tried to call her, but my cell doesn't work. I went to both entrances of the park, but her car wasn't there, so they may have gone somewhere else."

"So you decided to take Boxer out for a ride?" Maggie asked.

Joanna shook her head. "My car won't start."

They went into the shop and Joanna picked up the phone and listened for a dial tone. "I was hoping the land line would work." She began pressing in numbers. "It's ringing. Went to voice mail. Alex, call the shop. My cell phone doesn't work. There's been an earthquake or something. I hope you're on this side of the rift. It's all very weird. Call." She pushed the off button. "I'll try Jeri's number," she said to Maggie. "Kate? It's Joanna. Are Alex and Jeri back yet? Where'd they go? Oh man. Have you heard about what's happened? Yeah, yeah. Have her call the shop. A crash? What kind? No, I can't get on the internet and the only channel that works on the cable is the public access and it says 'stay tuned for more details.' But there haven't been any details. Okay. Thanks."

Joanna hung up the phone.

"Why don't you look reassured?" Maggie asked.

"They went hiking in Sabino Canyon."

On the other side of the rift.

"I bet she doesn't even know about the rift," Joanna said. She sat on the stool at the counter.

"Joanna," Maggie said. "We're okay, she's okay. If worse comes to worse, we'll get some kind of gangplank and throw it over the rift and she can come here or you can go there."

Joanna shook her head. "There's something more going on, Maggie. Kate said it's all over the news. There was some kind of crash in the Rincons. There is all kinds of speculation. Secret military plane. Terrorist plane. UFO."

"Come on," Maggie said. "There'd be military all over if that were the case."

Joanna shook her head. "They're not letting anyone come in or anyone go out. They're saying there's some kind of electrical disturbance so they can't fly into the area."

"If there was a crash, they'd figure out a way to get here. I'll get my binoculars and check it out."

Joanna nodded. "I'll stay here in case Alexandria calls."

Maggie pointed to the piece of paper on the counter with the phone number on it. "We're supposed to call that number if we have any questions."

Maggie ran into the house and retrieved her binoculars. Then she went to her car parked under the carport and tried to start it.

It didn't make a sound. Dead.

She got out of the car and looked over at Joanna who stood in the threshold of the shop with her arms folded.

"Just like mine," she said. "You can take Boxer."

Maggie put the binoculars over her head and off to the side. Then she went to Boxer's left flank and patted her. "Mind if we go for a spin?" Boxer turned her head and nuzzled her. Maggie got the reins, put her left foot in the stirrup as she grabbed the saddle horn and she pulled herself up and onto the horse.

The horse and Maggie went down the wash with Maggie watching for rattlesnakes. She didn't see anything moving. Today the desert seemed perfectly still. Still life. Frozen in place. Sometimes she thought of the desert as a 3-D portrait—even though she knew the desert was not motionless. It moved at its own pace.

Sometimes at dusk, with the setting sun behind her, Maggie looked to the east and the desert seemed to be moving toward her so slowly that it was almost spooky. Like a desert zombie movie. There was the saguaro rocking slightly this way and then that way toward her, only moving when her gaze was settled on something else. There were the teddy bear cholla, kicking up their prickly heels in a chorus dance, only shaking when she turned to look at the paloverde who whispered as it moved, "The answers are all here, here."

Maggie smiled now in the bright sunlight. She did not ordinarily think about zombies or anything supernatural when she considered the desert. She knew it was filled with a variety of wondrous creatures, some of them visible, some of them not so visible.

Maggie and Boxer reached the end of the wash at Fifth Avenue. Boxer seemed to know where Maggie wanted her to go. She headed east toward the park. They passed by Tilly and Bill's house. It was so far from the road, like most house in this area, that Maggie couldn't see much.

Several cars were parked around the park entrance. Maggie guessed none of them knew about the rift yet. She and Boxer went into the park and down a trail until Maggie had an unobstructed view of this side of the Rincon Mountains.

Boxer stopped when Maggie gently pulled on the reins. She looked through the binoculars. The sunlight was highlighting the saguaro growing on the sides of the distant mountains so that they looked like green stubble. A kind of cacti five o'clock shadow. She slowly looked up and down the mountains. She saw no signs of a crash or of rescuers traveling toward a crash.

"Come on, Boxer," Maggie said. "I think people are just making shit up." She nodded to the saguaro, the cholla, mesquite, and the jackrabbit watching her, and then she and Boxer left the park and headed in the direction of home.

The gate at the end of Tilly and Bill's driveway began to open as Boxer and Maggie trotted past. Maggie stopped Boxer and looked toward the house.

"Can you come in, Maggie?" Bill's voice came over the intercom. She was tempted to tease him, call him Dr. Strangelove or Hunter Thompson, but she decided against it. She turned Boxer, and they went down the drive. Pencil cholla and prickly pear cactus crowded the dirt road. She wondered how Bill and Tilly ever got their truck in and out it. Boxer didn't seem to notice. One of their horses whinnied and Boxer answered.

Near the house, Maggie stopped Boxer and got off. Bill came out of the house and took Boxer's reins. "Tilly wants to see you."

"Okay."

Maggie took off the binoculars and hung them on the saddle horn. Then she walked into the house.

"Hello!" she called as she went down a short dark hallway and into the living room. Tilly sat by the window with a quilt tucked around her.

"You cold?" Maggie asked. She went over to Tilly, kissed the top of her head, and gently rubbed her arms. "I'll warm you up."

"Sit," Tilly said.

Maggie pulled up a foot rest and sat close to Tilly. She looked into her eyes. Tilly had the brightest and clearest brown eyes, even when she didn't feel well. Tilly accepted the fact she was ill, accepted it much more than the people around her did, especially Bill. Maggie didn't like it much either, and she kept hoping Tilly would get better.

"Do you know what's happening?" Tilly asked.

"You mean about the rift?" Maggie asked. She put her hands on Tilly's knees and ran some healing energy.

"About everything," Tilly asked. "I assumed you journeyed on it and asked your helpers."

Maggie smiled. Tilly was one of the few people who understood that Maggie talked to the Invisibles. "I didn't," she said. "But you're right. I should have asked someone. It's been a very strange morning."

"Bill's talking about government conspiracies," she said.

"Naturally," Maggie said.

Tilly smiled.

"If I get worse, he wants me to go to the hospital," she said, "and now he's in a panic because they say no one can leave. I don't want to go to the hospital, so it's fine with me. Please, don't let him do anything crazy to get me to a hospital."

"Tilly, I have absolutely no sway with your husband," Maggie said. "He thinks I'm some flake walking around in the desert barefoot talking to the air."

"Do you go barefoot?"

"No," Maggie said. "I am not a crazy person."

"Sometimes I take off my shoes and dig my toes into the dirt," Tilly said. "Feels like going home."

"You are a crazy person." Maggie smiled. "I know what you mean. I do that sometimes, too."

"My plant spirit helper came to me in a dream last night," Tilly said.

Maggie nodded. Queen Anne's Lace. Not a desert plant. Maggie figured she showed up because Tilly had grown up in the Midwest.

"What'd she have to say?"

"She told me I was going to go on the ride of my life," she said. "I figure that means I'm going to die soon."

"Really? Is that what you felt like in the dream?"

"It felt like something was ending and something was beginning. She told me today was the day everything would change. So maybe today is the day."

Maggie felt a chill run down her spine.

"The wind told me that very same thing this morning," Maggie said.

The women looked at one another.

"I don't know, Tilly," Maggie said. "It doesn't feel like you're about to kick the bucket today."

"Everyone walks around acting like I'm some kind of saint," Tilly said. "I'm not. I'm just sick. That means I'm too tired to act like an asshole. I used to be like Bill, you know. Paranoid. Angry. He was the laid-back one, and then when I got sick our roles kind of switched."

"Tilly, I've known you for a decade," Maggie said. "You and Bill seem as different as night and day."

Tilly shook her head. "His heart broke when I got sick, that's all. So now he's stuck up in his head. No communication between the head and the heart."

"That happens to a lot of people," Maggie said. Much of the world, actually.

"This is what I think," Tilly said. "The story in the Bible about people getting expelled from Paradise is a true story. A metaphor, of course. But true. Something happened and we severed our link to nature and it has all been downhill from there. We've been looking for our true home since then."

"Someone once said that all sickness is homesickness," Maggie said.

Tilly nodded.

Maggie heard the front door open and close. A moment later Bill walked into the room.

"Bill, I'm saying this here now in front of a witness," Tilly said. "If I get worse or go into a coma or something, I don't want to go to a hospital. At least not while this rift is here. It would just be a mess."

"I'm not going to let you die because of some stupid crack in the road," Bill said.

"That would not be the reason I died," Tilly said. "I want to be here in my own home. With you."

Bill glanced at Maggie and then looked away.

"I wish you'd stop talking about dying," Bill said. "Isn't there something in all that New Age crap that says you have to be positive all the time?"

"I suppose that was directed at me," Maggie said. "And I can tell you that talking with the plants is definitely 'old age,' not New Age. And the idea that we need to be positive all the time is ludicrous. Every atom has a negative and a positive charge, so it seems to me we need both for a healthy life. Just like we need the darkness and the light."

"Oh man," Bill said. "I can't listen to this. I wish they'd get the cable fixed. Can't get anything but that stupid public access channel and all it says is 'stay tuned.'"

"He's had it on in his room all day," Tilly said.

Maggie dropped her hands from Tilly's knees and got up. "I better get back home. Call me if you need anything." She leaned over and kissed Tilly's cheek. She nodded to Bill. She thought about telling Tilly that Bill had wanted to shoot the crows earlier, but he gave her an almost a pleading look, and she decided to keep quiet. She went outside, got on Boxer, and headed home.

Maggie found Jack and Joanna in the shop after she left Boxer by the corrals. Joanna looked uncharacteristically pale and worried. Jack sat on the treatment table, looking clean and refreshed after his shower and change of clothes. He grinned when Maggie walked in the door, and the hair on the back of her neck stood up.

"Don't I clean up purty?" Jack asked.

"Uh, sure," Maggie said.

"Aw shucks, ma'am."

Maggie sighed in exasperation. She really did not know what to say to this man.

"Did you see anything?" Joanna asked.

Maggie shook her head, then took the binoculars off and set them on the counter.

"I tried that number over and over," Joanna said. "It's busy. Ricardo stopped by and he's tried, too. Kate hasn't heard from Jeri and Alex yet, but she thought they'd be hiking for a while. Alex didn't think I was going to be home until five, after I finished with my last client."

Maggie patted her friend's arm.

"Honey, it's okay," she said. "Everyone is all right."

"I feel trapped here," Joanna said. "I can't go to town. I can't get groceries. Can't drive my car."

"Isn't it great?" Jack said. "It's so still and calm. You could hear a feather drop."

"I don't think it's great," Joanna said. "I did, when I thought Alexandria was on this side."

"Since we can't get any answers on the phone, internet, or television," Maggie said, "let's see if that real live person will tell us anything. Let's go out to the rift."

"I want to stay here in case Alex calls," Joanna said.

Maggie nodded. She glanced over at Jack.

"So you coming or what?"

Jack slid off the table. He was so tall it didn't take much before he could stand. Together Maggie and Jack walked out into the sunshine. Maggie headed toward the wash.

"Aren't we taking the horse?" he asked. "We could ride double. Pressed up against one another during this time of trial and tribulation. Wouldn't it be fun?"

"One trial and tribble at a time," Maggie said. She stepped into the wash and headed north, toward John and Nina's house. They wouldn't care if she cut across their property.

"What's your hurry?" Jack asked as he caught up with her. "It's the desert. Slow down and smell the mesquite."

"Still a little wobbly?" Maggie asked.

Jack didn't say anything.

"Yeah, walking on this sand isn't the best thing for someone with a hangover," Maggie said. "You want to turn back and wait with Joanna?"

"I'm wise to your ways, Mags," he said. "You ain't gonna dump me that easily."

The wash skirted John and Nina's property and flowed out onto Speedway. Once again Maggie turned left and headed west down the road toward the flashing lights. She could see Ricardo's truck parked near the rift. Why was his truck working? Maybe because it was so old and didn't have as much electrical equipment to fry. If that was what had happened to the other vehicles.

As they got closer, Maggie could see several of their neighbors gathered at the rift, including John and Nina.

Jack and Maggie got to the edge of the crowd and heard Jeff Shaw saying something about emergency rations.

"Emergency rations?" Maggie said. "It's been three hours."

John and Nina turned around.

"Hey, how it's going?" John asked. He looked at Jack. Jack held out his hand.

"Coyote Jack, friend," he said. "At your service."

"I'm John and this is Nina," John said as he shook Jack's hand. "You a visitor who got caught on this side?"

"Why can't you tell us what happened?" Maggie heard Lisa's voice. Maggie walked around the crowd so that she was standing at the rift. Jack followed.

"Far out," Jack said as he looked down at the rift. "Never seen nothing like this before."

"I've told you all I know," Shaw said.

A ways down Speedway, Maggie saw lots of cars and trucks. Probably camera crews.

"Then we need to talk with someone who knows more," Lisa said. "And if it's so safe, why are you keeping everyone away from us?"

"We don't want people trying to cross," he said.

"Why don't we have cell service?" Maggie asked. "Or internet access. Why aren't our cars working?"

"We don't know," Shaw said. "It is probably all coincidence. Seems like today is a perfect storm for everything to go wrong."

"I'd call that an imperfect storm," Lisa said. "I want to see some people out here fixing the road. That seems to be the big thing."

"It's Sunday," he said. "We're having trouble getting road crews. The rift is long."

"That sounds like a bullshit excuse," Lisa said. "You can get road crews out any time of the night or day."

"Ma'am," Shaw said. "We are doing the best we can."

Shaw looked right at them when he talked. He wasn't offended by Lisa's anger. He didn't seem to care. Maggie had assumed he was some kind of bureaucrat, but now she felt certain he was the guy in charge. And for some reason, they wanted everyone on the east side to stay on the east side.

The crowd began to disperse. Maggie's friends gathered over by Ricardo's truck. Maggie waited until most everyone was out of hearing range. Then she said to Shaw, "Has there been some kind of nuclear accident?"

Shaw looked at her. "Absolutely not," he said.

She looked into his eyes.

"But you think we've been contaminated with something?"

"I do not think you've been contaminated by anything," he said.

"You don't," she said. "But do scientists or anyone else?"

"We have no reason to believe any of you has been exposed to radiation or any toxic chemicals or substances. The ground is unsteady and could shift again. And there are some strange electrical disturbances happening which we can't quite explain. For now, we think it would be better if people stayed home. If we temporarily fixed this road and everyone left and then it shifted again and was even worse, then everyone would be stuck on this side screaming about getting home. If this takes more than a day, we'll figure out a way to get supplies in."

Maggie looked at Jeff Shaw and he looked at her.

Everything he said sounded plausible. She heard a crow call out. She followed the sound and looked to her left at a grove of trees that ran along Freeman, on this side of the rift. She saw the crow that had called out. And she saw another. And another. The trees were filled with crows. Thousands of them. They looked like black blossoms on the winter bare trees. All of them faced west. Here and there, one or two would leap up and fly away a bit and land on another tree. They flew south, north, east. They did not cross the rift.

Maggie looked back at Shaw. He didn't say anything.

Maggie turned around and started walking east down Speedway.

"Five o'clock at our house!" Lisa called to her. "Be there or be on my shit list."

"You'd never know," Maggie called. "The list is too long!" She waved.

"Potluck!" Lisa shouted.

Jack ran to catch up with Maggie.

"Did you see the crows?" she asked.

"Sure," he said. "Isn't that something? Probably come to see the show tonight."

"What show?"

"You know, full moon lunar eclipse. The fun is just starting, Mags."

"Don't call me that," Maggie said. "Makes me sound like I'm a wheel or a pile of magazines."

"I think it's perfect," Jack said. "Short for magnificent!"

Maggie groaned and kept on walking.

NEXT

By the time Maggie got back to the shop, she had lost Jack, which made her happy, and Joanna had heard from Alexandria. Alex had tried to drive to the rift, but the police had turned her back. She was staying with Kate and Jeri until she could get across again. Monday she'd try to find out more. Alex was a lawyer; she was good at sussing out the facts, and she would find out whether the city had the legal authority to keep people from crossing the rift.

"You can stay in my spare bedroom until Alex gets home if you want," Maggie suggested.

"I've got the cats to take care of," Joanna said. "And Boxer is happiest when she's home with Crazy Lu." Alex's horse.

"You going to Lisa and Ricardo's for dinner?" Maggie asked.

"Sure," Joanna said. "I'll go home and whip up something."

After Joanna and Boxer left, Maggie went to the bunkhouse and knocked on the door. When no one answered, she went inside. Coyote Jack had made the bed and put his pile of clothes away. She glanced around. Nothing of value anyone could steal or hurt themselves on. She got the key from the cupboard and put it on the bed. Until he left, this was now Jack's space and she had no rights to it, as far as she was concerned.

She left the bunkhouse and went into the shop. She loved walking into this space. It felt homey, relaxed, welcoming. She ran her fingers over the rocks as she walked around the room. She didn't keep live plants in the shop because she thought it only fair that plants live in the ground. Having them in pots was too much like looking at animals in cages. It wasn't right. She wasn't too sure about this riding horses thing either, even though Alex and Joanna and all the other horse people she knew insisted the horses liked to be ridden.

"With a piece of metal in their mouths?" Maggie always asked. And when she wanted to know how they could be sure the horses liked it, her friends would invariably says to her, "How do you know what the plants are saying?"

She had become friends with Boxer and Crazy Lu. Even though she wouldn't swear they liked be ridden, she was fairly certain they liked the company as they went from here to there.

She still didn't think they liked a bit in their mouths.

She looked around the shop. Why was she here? She shrugged. She grabbed the laptop and then left and went into her house.

For the potluck, she made a warm salad with rice

noodles, thinly sliced shitake mushrooms, and steamed vegetables.

It was nearly five o'clock when she finished. Five o'clock and nothing new or strange had happened in the last hour or so. Maybe nothing else was going to happen. Maybe the rift was it. Just a break in the earth. Happened all the time.

She put the salad in a Pyrex bowl, pressed a top over it, and went outside. The day was still warm and sunny but the desert felt a bit more energetic, as it often did when dusk was near. Twilight was when the hunting began. When flora and fauna shook off the dust of day and became full of their true wild selves.

At least, that was how it felt to Maggie.

She walked down the drive, then the dirt road. She turned right on Speedway and walked to the next road. Turned right and went a little ways until she came to Ricardo's driveway. She could hear voices coming from inside the low adobe house as her feet crunched over the peach-colored desert dirt. The jalapeño Christmas lights flashed off and on.

Maggie knocked on the metal door and then let herself in. Her neighbors had gathered in the kitchen and were overflowing into the dining/living room. She put her salad on the table and then looked around for Joanna. Didn't see her.

The rooms felt close—too many people crowded together. She took a deep breath. She had forgotten to prepare herself before she walked into a room full of people. Rookie mistake. She quickly let herself out the back door. Stepped into the cooler outdoors. Breathed deeply. She walked over to the tall paloverde and put her hand on its green trunk.

"Thank you, thank you," she said.

Beyond her, Alicia and her friend Carola pulled apart a hay bale to feed the horses.

Maggie pressed her spine up against the tree. "If you don't mind."

She breathed again.

"How about a drink?"

She turned. Jack held a bottle in each hand. "One for you," he said. "Don't give me that look. These are Joanna's homemade ginger ale. Don't you recognize them? Nothing hard. Only agave as sweetener."

Maggie took the proffered bottle.

"How come I'd never seen you before Ricardo brought you over, I mean, if you've been working for Ricardo for a while?"

Jack shrugged. He leaned over and touched the paloverde trunk. Maggie moved out of the way.

"I apologize," Jack said. "Felt an urge to touch the tree. Something sensuous about paloverde trees. Like green snake women. You remember that episode on the old *Star Trek*. Was it with Captain Pike? They were on some kind of pleasure planet and this woman dancer was green and snake-like. Or maybe tree-like for all we know."

Maggie made a noise. Jack was right; there was something sensuous about the paloverde. But when he said it, it sounded sleazy.

"I heard this thing once about people," Jack said. "Our hearts are actually the center of our bodies, but somehow we got to thinking that the truth came from our thoughts, and that's probably how we lost our connection to the natural world. Every *thing* and every *one* is communicating with us through their hearts, but we don't know it cuz we're caught in this cage in our heads. But, we can fix it. We can stand close to each other, or this tree, and our hearts will get in sync after awhile. I think they call it entrainment."

Maggie and Jack moved until they were standing about a foot from each other and the tree.

"That's right," Maggie said. "That's what I do when I go out into the desert with the plants. When I first started doing this work I read a book, by Stephen Buhner, I think. He said just be near a plant and ask it how it's doing, and then see how you feel. After a while, you'll notice something different from each plant. It's not words, but it is a kind of communication."

"So let's do it," Jack said.

"Do what?"

"Entrain our hearts to each other. Seems like the neighborly thing to do, doesn't it?"

"All right," Maggie said.

They stood face to face. She breathed deeply. Jack still smelled a little of alcohol. She didn't look at him. She just wanted to feel his energy.

"How are you?" she thought to herself.

She felt a wave of grief again.

After a moment, he asked, "Are we in sync now?"

"I suppose so," she said. "Like friends."

Jack nodded. "Like friends."

She heard the back door open. Ricardo leaned out and said, "Come and get it."

Alicia and Carola ran past them. Maggie patted the tree to say good-bye, and then she headed for the house, with Jack behind her.

Maggie found Joanna and sat next to her. While they ate, people took turns talking about what they had heard.

Mostly people repeated rumors: The rift was a government experiment gone bad, nuclear meltdown from a secret facility, toxic spill, terrorist, or plane crash.

Joanna mentioned that she had spoken to Alex. "Alex has been watching the news, and they're reporting that it was an earthquake with lots of aftershocks. That's why they're not repairing the road."

"I never felt nothing," Ricardo said, "and no aftershocks."

Everyone started talking at once. Joanna leaned over to Maggie and whispered. "You wanted us to start getting together as a community again," she said. "Guess you got your wish."

Maggie nodded.

"Hey, Ricardo," Wendell Davies said. "How come your truck works? I can't get any of my cars or trucks to work. No one else can either."

Ricardo shrugged. "How do I know? Our car doesn't work. My tractor works fine though, if someone wants to borrow it. Anyone else try their tractor?"

"What about you, space lady?" Wendell again, addressing Nina. "You seen any of those aliens lately? I mean the kind from outer space, not you, Ricardo."

The room got very quiet.

"Listen, you little pinhead." Lisa stood and faced Wendell. Maggie smiled. Ah, Mr. Wendell Davies had no idea what he had just stepped into. "You are in my house and when you are in my house you will treat people with respect. The space lady has a name and it is Nina Levinson. You want me to spell that for you? And as far as aliens go, my husband's family has been here longer than any of you Anglo-Saxon assholes, so be careful who you are calling an alien."

"You people can't take a joke," Wendell said. "Always wrapped up in your bullshit political correctness."

"I'm gonna shove some—"

Maggie stood. "Excuse me. Isn't it a little early to be calling each other names? Didn't we want to get together so we could organize in case this goes on for a while? Help each other out. See who needs food and medicine. Stuff like that?"

"We've got paper on the table," Joanna said. "You can write down your grocery and medical needs there. We'll take it to the rift tomorrow and see what we can do since nobody's been able to get through on that phone number they gave us."

"There are some people stuck up at the park," John said, "but we knocked on doors earlier and got everyone a room. We've got a nice couple from Brooklyn staying with us."

"Who has enough food for a few days?" Maggie asked.

"If our electricity holds out," Lisa said, "we can go for a week. If the electricity fails, we're screwed."

"We've got a backup generator," Ricardo said, "and an extra freezer. Anyone is free to store food in there if the electricity goes out."

"How would we cook it if they have no electricity?" someone asked.

"Good old barbecue," someone else answered.

The mood lightened. People began talking amongst themselves and eating again.

"What time's the eclipse?" someone asked. Maggie didn't recognize the voice or see the person.

"About 8:00," Joanna answered. She stood. "I'm going now. I want to get home before dark."

Other people began getting up and preparing to leave.

"I can give anyone a ride," Ricardo said.

"Shouldn't you save your gasoline for emergencies?" Maggie asked.

"I converted it," he said. "It runs on biofuel."

"I had completely forgotten that," Maggie said. "Maybe that's why it's still running."

"It's still the same kind of engine," Ricardo said. "Just very old!"

Lisa took Maggie by the arm and pulled her aside. "You be careful tonight. That Jack could come after you in your sleep."

"Did he do anything like that while he was staying here?" Maggie asked.

"No," Lisa said. She shrugged. "He drank and cried, cried and drank. Walked the wash. I like my men with more cojones, you know. I wanted to smack him all the time. Got on my nerves."

Maggie laughed. "I'll see you later, Lisa. Thanks for having this."

As Maggie tried to make her way to the door, people kept stopping to talk with her. By the time she got outside, it was dark. She could see the glow of the moon coming up behind the Rincon Mountains as she headed for home. Lights continued to flash on the police cruisers parked on the other side of the rift. She was tempted to go down and see what news they had, but they probably had no news. She turned down her road.

"Mind some company?" Jack was suddenly beside her.

"Where'd you come from?" she asked.

"I've been trying to catch up to you since Ricardo's," Jack said.

Maggie remembered Lisa's warning. Maybe she was right. Jack could be violent. He might be a serial killer. How did people figure out these kinds of things? She and Jack had stood face to face. She had felt the energy of his heart—his electromagnetic field. She had felt grief, not violence.

At least, that was what she thought she felt.

They walked down the drive and stepped into the wash just as the light of the full moon spilled over the mountains and down on them. Maggie stopped and turned to face the moon. She felt the sand beneath the soles of her feet as she watched the moon. She heard Jack breathing next to her.

"By the light of the silvery moon," he sang quietly.

Maggie heard a whisper. She looked to her right down the wash, in the direction the rattlesnakes had taken earlier in the day. Moonlight washed the sand in silver so that it looked like snow. And on the moon-created snow, a group of jackrabbits shimmered. That was the only word Maggie could think of to describe their appearance. They *shimmered.*

Probably twenty of them. Many of them half stood so that they looked almost human—or elf-like—stretching in the moonlight. Thin and lanky, so different from their cousins, the cottontails. Their bodies seemed more coyote than rabbit. The jackrabbits reached out a paw here and there, companionably, to the other jackrabbits. Their long ears looked more preternatural than usual. Normally Maggie let the wild be the wild and didn't try to insert herself where she didn't belong. But she wanted to get closer, be closer, and find out what they were doing, why they looked almost phosphorescent.

She glanced at Jack. "Do you see them?" she whispered.

He nodded. "Some kind of mad hatter tea party?"

Maggie frowned.

"You know, like in *Alice in Wonderland.*"

"Ah."

Maggie began walking slowly and quietly toward the group. She could feel Jack behind her. The wash unraveled before her like a silver stream winding through the desert, curving here and there to avoid the mesquite or a prickly pear patch. Beyond the jackrabbits, something big and dark moved. She hoped it wasn't a predator. And beyond it, more shimmering.

Maggie felt a little dizzy. She looked up. The shadow of the Earth was taking a bite out of the moon.

The eclipse. Maggie had almost forgotten about the eclipse.

She looked around. The entire desert seemed to be aglow. Phosphorescent. Shimmering.

Something.

She looked behind her.

Where was Jack?

The jackrabbits suddenly stopped and looked at her. She froze. They froze. Then as a group they looked south, away from her. The dark shape was moving toward them.

They began leaping away. It reminded Maggie of grasshoppers fleeing as she walked through a field of grass when she was a girl growing up in Michigan. Only these were giant grasshoppers.

No, Maggie, jackrabbits.

The dark shape was coming toward her.

Maggie tried to leap, but she didn't have the legs for it. She stepped back just as the shape—the thing—thundered by her.

A horse. She was fairly certain it was a horse.

Then it was gone.

Still, something glowed in the wash.

And maybe moaned. Or cried. Maggie called on her spirit helpers to protect her.

She walked toward the figure. It was shaped like a person, although she could only see the outline of it. Its arms seemed to be flailing.

Then it collapsed. Fell onto the sand. And the light went out.

Maggie ran toward it. Even as she ran, she thought she was crazy. She could be running toward a bear, a cougar, a crazy coyote, a rabid anything.

It was difficult running in the wash. It was like running on a sandy beach. Or like running in a dream.

But soon she dropped down onto the sand next to what looked like a very thin man.

A very thin and naked man. His face was buried in the sand.

She pulled on his shoulder to turn him over. He moved easily, as though he was much lighter than he should or could be. Long light-colored hair hung down over his face.

"Sir?" Maggie said. "Hello. Sir. Are you all right?"

She touched his arm. It was cold and her hand instinctively jerked away.

She made herself touch him again. "Sir, you can't stay here. You'll freeze to death."

The temperature had already dropped drastically

from only an hour ago. Maggie wished she had brought her jacket.

She felt the man's wrist for his pulses. They felt strange, but he was alive.

She couldn't get him up by herself.

"Jack!" she called. "Jack!"

"I'm right here." She heard Jack's voice but couldn't see him. A few moments later she heard his feet on the sand. Then he dropped down beside her.

"Where'd you go?" she asked.

"I don't know," he said. "It got all weird, and I couldn't find you. I swear I just saw a unicorn or some kind of strange horse. And the jackrabbits turned into giant grasshoppers. Who is this?"

"I have no idea," Maggie said. "He seems to be passed out."

"A fellow drinker?"

"I don't smell anything. Can you help me get him up? We better put him someplace warm."

Together they lifted the man.

"Whoa!" Jack said. "He is light. Practically floats. And lookie here. His skin is shiny or see-through. Something weird."

"It's just the moonlight," Maggie said. Which was nearly gone as the eclipse continued. "Let's get him back before we're in total darkness."

Maggie heard a growl. She looked around. Didn't see anything. Another growl.

She sighed. "I don't have time for this." She growled back. Then she and Jack hurried through the wash toward her house, carrying the unconscious man between them. When they got to the barn, Maggie unlocked the shop, and they carried the man to the treatment table and

 KIM ANTIEAU

gently put him on it. Maggie got a blanket from beneath the table and dropped it over the man. Then she turned on a small lamp on the counter.

The man groaned.

Maggie and Jack glanced at one another and then back at the man.

He was strange looking. He was not as tall as Maggie had originally thought. Not as tall as Jack. Maybe Maggie's height, but thinner. And his skin was . . . translucent. His hair was long, fine, and blond.

"Maybe Nina was right," Jack said. "Maybe the aliens landed and this here is one of them."

Maggie shook her head. "No, he's just a person. He's probably cold."

Maggie grounded herself, and then she went to the end of the table. She gently put her hands on the man's head. She felt a shock of static electricity. She closed her eyes. The tips of her fingers tingled. She opened herself to allow the healing energy to flow down and through her: She was a hollow bone.

She felt as though she was floating. And then she was in the desert riding a dark blue horse over a golden landscape bathed in moonlight. Tall saguaro marched alongside them. Prickly pear clapped their prickly pads together. A jackrabbit leaped across the path in front of them. Ahead was a rip in the fabric of the night. Milky stars spilled through the tear, along with a variety of creatures Maggie did not recognize. And then she realized the shimmering man was one of them. Disoriented, he covered his face. She said to herself, "It's all right. You're all right. Just turn around and go back." But the rip disappeared. The man walked up to her. She reached her hand down. He took it and somehow got up onto the horse, behind her, close to her, and she leaned back, as she would naturally lean back into the most comfortable place in the universe.

Maggie opened her eyes. That was the most vivid journey she had ever experienced. More like a dream, or ordinary life. The man opened his eyes. They were red, for an instant, and then green. He smiled at her, then closed his eyes again.

Maggie took her hands off of the man. Jack started to say something, but Maggie put her finger up to her lips. They left the room and stepped outside. She shut the door quietly behind her. The eclipse was over; the moon was much higher in the sky.

"As my old grandpa used to say: That was very very very weird," Jack said.

"Your grandfather used to say that?" Maggie said.

"Yep, his very words."

Maggie rubbed her face. "This has been a strange night."

"Not the night," he said. "That." He pointed to the door to Desert Bloomers. "Do you know how long you stood there with your hands on him?"

"About five minutes," she said.

"An hour or more," he said. "I was about ready to pull you off of him."

"Healing sessions can take an hour or more," she said. She felt as though she was going to fall to sleep standing up. She rubbed her head again. "I think I need to go to sleep. Jack, can you do me a favor? Will you check on him now and again?"

"Yeah, sure," Jack said. "You okay?"

"Just really tired," she said. "Sometimes happens."

Maggie wasn't sure how she did it, but she got into her house and found her bed and fell onto it.

NEXT

Maggie awakened, dreamless, to midday. She knew it was midday because of the way the light came through her blinds, not because she had a clock in her room. She didn't. She didn't have a clock anywhere in the house except on the oven, and that one didn't keep accurate time.

Maggie had decided long ago that she would not be a slave to a clock. She wanted to follow the motions of the planet and the land. Despite this, she almost always knew what time it was—or maybe because of it. She was never late for an appointment with a client.

Today, she opened her eyes and remembered what had happened yesterday—the rift—and what had happened last night in the wash.

Last night she had felt catatonic. This morning, she felt energized.

She practically jumped out of bed, took a quick shower, and then got dressed. She was humming as she came out of the bathroom. She walked into the kitchen and found Joanna sitting at her kitchen table. Joanna looked over at her and smiled.

"Have a late night?" Joanna asked.

"Not especially," Maggie said.

"The water in the kettle is hot," Joanna said. "And I put beans and rice in the oven for you."

Maggie poured hot water into a mug, then used a mitten to take the plate out of the oven. She carried both over to the table—along with a fork—then sat down and started eating.

"I met Anders," Joanna said. "I brought over breakfast for you and Jack, but you were sleeping, so Anders got yours."

"Who is Anders?"

"Your fey fellow," Joanna said. "I examined him, since he was acting a little odd. Doesn't seem to know his last name and he keeps saying he's from here. I've never seen him before. All of his reflexes are fine. His pupils are reacting to light properly, so I don't think there's a head injury. Jack said you found him in the wash. Along with some kind of strange horse. And jackrabbits."

"We didn't find the jackrabbits," Maggie said. "They were just hanging out in the moonlight."

Joanna gave her a look.

"Hey, I just woke up," Maggie said. "I don't know what's going on yet."

"What's going on is that there's still a rift," Joanna said. "The cellphones still don't work. And the latest thing is that they're asking all nonresidents to go to one particular place."

"Nonresidents?" Maggie asked between mouthfuls. She was famished. She couldn't believe how hungry she was. "Is that a euphemism for 'undocumented aliens'?"

"It could be," Joanna said, "but they said they were talking about people who had been hiking in the parks. They want to figure out a way to get them home. They don't think they can fix the road today. Plus, apparently some people are missing. They're worried some of the missing might be in the rift. So they want to account for everyone."

"Is anyone out working on the road?"

Joanna shook her head, then took a gulp of coffee. Maggie had never developed a taste for coffee. She sipped her hot water.

"Anders?" Maggie said. "Did he tell you his name was Anders?"

"Jack did," Joanna said. "He's been asking for you, by the way, this Anders fellow. I suppose since he's a nonresident he should go to the house."

"What house?"

"Hey, if you're going to sleep away half the day, you're going to miss things," Joanna said. "There's a particular house they've told people to meet at. It's off Broadway near Freeman. I guess the people who own it work for the City of Tucson, and they're out of town and they gave permission to the city to use it for nonresidents. Apparently."

Maggie shook her head. "That seems very odd."

Joanna shrugged. "If they can take the nonresidents back over the rift, then Alex can come home, right?"

"Did I leave the front door unlocked?" Maggie asked.

"You did indeed," Joanna said. "I figured with Jack running around you would have locked your house up good."

Maggie pushed the empty plate away. "Yeah, you'd think."

Maggie and Joanna left the house and headed to the barn. Maggie heard voices. She followed the sound and found Jack and the man from the wash sitting in chairs on the bunkhouse porch, looking out at the desert.

The man from the wash did not look quite as frail or as strange in the daylight. He was wearing blue jeans and a plaid shirt.

"I went home and got him some of Alex's clothes," Joanna said. "From when she used to dress like a boy." She smiled.

The man stood when he saw Maggie and Joanna. An instant later, Jack stood, too. Maggie stepped up onto the porch and held out her hand to the man. He took it between both of his hands. She felt a tiny shock of static electricity again.

"Thank you, Maggie," he said. His voice sounded peculiar, accented, yet not quite. He said her name as though there was a space between "mag" and "gee."

"You are welcome," Maggie said. "Joanna said your name is Anders." She didn't know why but she spoke to him as though he wasn't quite all there—or like she would speak to a child. Yet he was no child. He was a tall, gorgeous hunk of man.

She shook her head.

She didn't normally think those kinds of things about people.

But he was good looking. Or something. She did not want him to let go of her hand.

"Yes, Anders," he said. "Maggie, I would like to return now."

"Return?" Maggie asked. "You mean to where we found you last night?"

"Yes, please," he said.

Maggie looked at Jack. He shrugged.

"Of course," Maggie said.

The man kept hold of her hand as they stepped off the porch and walked down the drive. Jack and Joanna followed. They all turned south in the wash. The wash looked so ordinary today, making last night seem like a dream.

They walked a ways and then Maggie stopped.

"I think it was here," she said. She looked at Jack. "Do you think?"

"Seems about right to me," he said, "but I think I was drunk on moonshine." He pointed upward. "The kind of moonshine that comes with a blue moon eclipse."

Maggie let go of Anders's hand. He looked around. For a moment he seemed frail again. Or not of this world. Maggie couldn't quite put her finger on what was different about him.

"It's gone," he said.

He began to cry. Maggie could not remember the last time she had seen a man cry. She put her hand on his arm.

"What's gone?" Maggie asked.

Jack put his arm across Anders's shoulders. "It's all right, buddy. We'll figure it out."

"Can you send me back?" he asked.

"I don't know what you mean," Maggie said.

Anders looked directly into her eyes. She could almost feel his body against hers, the way it had been when they had ridden the horse in her vision—as though his body had been a cushion of air or light.

But now she did not know what he wanted from her.

"He could have come from the rift," Jack suggested. "Maybe we should take him there."

Maggie felt momentarily queasy. No, they shouldn't go to the rift. Not yet. She wasn't sure anyone should know Anders was here.

"Let's do that later," Maggie said. "Joanna, could you call Alex and see if they have a list of the nonresidents or missing people? See if Anders's name is on there but don't say his name."

Joanna frowned.

"Just for now," Maggie said, "let's keep his existence between the three of us."

"Okay," Joanna said. "I'll go call."

"Do you live in one of the houses off the wash?" Maggie asked Anders.

She knew everyone in her neighborhood, she thought, but maybe he was a relative of a neighbor. Anders looked confused. Maggie led him down the wash a bit and pointed to one of the houses up away from the wash.

"Do you live there?" Maggie asked.

Anders shook his head. Then he walked up out of the wash and over to a saguaro with four limbs pointing skyward. He put his arms around the saguaro.

"Hey!" Maggie and Jack both cried out at the same time. They ran toward him, but it was too late: He was hugging the saguaro with his face and arms pressed into the thorns. He didn't look distressed or injured. He stayed that way for a bit.

Then he let go of the saguaro and turned around.

Not a drop of blood on him and no thorns stuck to him.

"I know what happened," he said. His voice sounded stronger. He had less of an accent now. "I have to wait until it happens again."

"What happens again?" Jack asked.

Anders pointed to the sky. Maggie and Jack both looked up.

"The eclipse?" Maggie asked. Another eclipse would occur on the New Moon in two weeks.

"I am hungry," Anders said. "May I have more food?" He smiled at both of them. It was the smile of a mischievous child.

Maggie laughed. "Sure," she said, "but I'm not much of a cook."

"I am," Jack said.

"You are?" Maggie asked as the three of them began walking back toward the house.

"Yes, I am," Jack said. "Why do you think Lisa let me stay at the house so long?"

Maggie heard machinery. She turned around and saw Joan Doud's handy man, Gabriel, coming down the wash on his little tractor.

Maggie turned back to Anders and Jack. "Go on in my house and use my kitchen," Maggie said. "Use whatever you like."

Jack took the hint that she didn't want Gabriel to see Anders. He steered Anders up and out of the wash. Maggie turned back to Gabriel. She waved and walked toward him. He got off the tractor and began pulling barbed wire and metal fence posts off the back of the tractor as it continued to sputter and spew diesel fumes.

"What's going on?" Maggie shouted above the noise.

"Miss Doud wants a fence up," Gabriel said.

"Why?"

He shrugged.

"That's all you know?" she said

"That's all I know."

Maggie hurried down the wash in the direction of Joan's house, away from her own. Once Maggie spotted Joan's house, she crossed the wash and went through the desert, past the corrals, and knocked on Joan's back door.

A minute passed and no one came. She knocked again. Another minute went by. Maggie pounded. Finally Joan opened the wooden door but kept the screen door shut between them. She held a drink in one hand and a metal poker in the other.

"Oh, it's you, Maggie," she said. "I thought some intruder was coming after me." She didn't set the poker down.

"Joan, Gabriel's down there putting up a fence in the wash," Maggie said. "What's that all about?"

"I'm tired of trespassers traipsing through my property," she said. "Last night you should have heard the ruckus! I have to protect myself."

"Joan, that wash has been a community right of way for decades," Maggie said. "Maybe even centuries. Putting a fence across it is like putting a fence across a river."

"It is my property," she said.

"But we all share the wash," Maggie said. "You can walk on my part of the wash. You can ride your horses.

Same with John and Nina's property. Now no one can ride their horses through the wash to get to the park."

Joan looked at her, her expression blank.

"I don't think you can do this legally," Maggie said. "We've got history on our side."

"Then sue me," Joan said.

"I can't get a lawyer now," Maggie said. "We're all stuck on this side. Wouldn't you rather work with us?"

Joan said, "I've already told you that I don't like what I see coming and going in that wash. I'm putting up a fence to let people know what's mine is mine. Now if there's nothing else, I have things to do."

"What about the coyotes?" Maggie asked, "and the bobcats. Mountain lions."

"If they know what's good for them, they'll go around," she said. "When you leave, go out the front to the road. I wouldn't want you to get hurt on my property."

With that, she shut the door. Maggie heard the lock turn. And then another lock.

Maggie made a noise. Then she went back into the wash by the same route she had taken to get there.

"What about the water?" Maggie mumbled to herself. "You gonna try to stop the water? Accuse it of trespassing?"

She tramped by Gabriel.

"This is ridiculous," she said. "And outrageous."

"What?"

Maggie reached across the tractor and turned it off.

"This fence is a terrible idea."

Gabriel shrugged and pushed one of the fence posts into the ground. "What can I do? She's the boss."

"She hasn't been in this wash in years," Maggie said. "What does she care who walks in the wash?"

"You know that she worries about those illegal aliens," he said. "She used to ask for my papers every other week. Until I told her if she keeps asking, I'm gonna charge her more. And then I asked her where she's from. You know her husband is from Saudi Arabia or some place like that."

Maggie started to walk away. "Hey, Gabriel, do you live here, on this side of the rift?"

He shook his head.

"They want all nonresidents to leave," she said.

"Yeah, but Miss Doud told me I could sleep in the bunkhouse. It's pretty nice there. And I don't have to listen to the kids or the wife."

"You tell Miss Doud if she puts up this fence I'm going to tell them you're staying at her place and you don't live there."

Gabriel hit the top of the fence post with a hammer. One, two, three times. He glanced at Maggie and then looked away.

"You go ahead," he said. "She'll just find someone else to put in the fence. She's a scared lady."

Maggie made a noise. "You know I wouldn't say anything to anyone about you. I can't believe I even said that out loud."

He shrugged. "Tough times all around."

When Maggie got to her property, she could hear Jack and Anders inside her house talking. She went into Desert Bloomers. Joanna was just putting down the phone. She looked tired.

"Whatever is going on," Joanna said, "they're not telling anyone. Alex is trying to get information out of any official she can bribe, browbeat, or coerce. No one is saying anything. And there's no one called Anders. Not even an Anderson."

"Joan Doud is putting a fence across the wash," Maggie said.

"What? Are you kidding me?" Joanna said. "That's like putting a fence across a river. What kind of crazy person does that?"

"Exactly my words," Maggie said. "I went to talk to her, but she was not receptive. Can she legally put up a fence in a wash that's been used for public access for decades?"

"I don't know," Joanna said. "Alex is the lawyer. Why is she doing it now?"

"I guess all the commotion last night scared her," Maggie said. "She thinks illegal aliens are stalking her."

"With Anders she might have a point. He is a bit alien-looking."

"I'm going down to the rift and see if I can find out anything," Maggie said.

This time she got her bike and pedaled down the driveway, the dirt road, and then onto Speedway. She headed toward the dark gash in the roadway. No one from the neighborhood stood on this side. Across the rift, the cop cars were still parked at an angle, lights still flashing. They had added yellow police "do not cross" tape that went from one end of the rift to the other, at least as far as Maggie could see.

Jeff Shaw got out of his car and walked toward the rift as she approached.

"What's this I hear about you gathering up all the nonresidents?" Maggie asked. No greeting, no small talk. The fence in the wash had obliterated any remaining mellowness she had, at least for today.

"We want to get them home," he said.

"But I thought you said no one could cross the rift," Maggie said. "Why aren't you repairing these roads? Can't you build a quick and dirty bridge? Then people could come and go. Why all this secrecy? Why the delay? We've got people who need to go to work, who have doctor appointments, who need food, medicine. What is the hold up?"

"Miss Maggie—what's your last name?" He looked down at his clipboard. Maggie bit her lip.

"What does it matter who I am?" Maggie said. "It is the responsibility of the City of Tucson to fix our roads. We pay taxes for just that thing."

"We are doing all we can," he said. "The state is now the lead agency. Engineers are assessing the damage and the danger all up and down the rift even as we speak."

Maggie looked north and she looked south.

"I don't see anyone," she said.

"Think of this like you would any disaster," he said. "It takes time for the relief agencies to get into place. It takes time for people to send food, water, and clothes."

"What are you talking about?" Maggie said. "This isn't Hurricane Katrina. This isn't a giant earthquake or a tsunami. There's a crack in the road. Fix it and we can be on our way."

Shaw hugged the clipboard to his chest. He walked closer to the rift. He glanced around, then motioned her closer. She came and stood at her edge of the rift.

"We don't want to frighten anyone," he said quietly. "But there's a possibility this was man-made. Some kind of terrorist plot. It's possible the entire rift is rigged with explosives that will go off once we start the repairs."

Maggie looked down into the abyss. She shook her head.

"We've already heard the terrorist plot theory," Maggie said. "It looks like an earthquake. Don't you have equipment to determine that?"

"An explosion can look just like an earthquake," Shaw said. "It's also possible that they've released something onto the east side of the rift. Some of our equipment have detected a kind of barrier coming out over the rift."

Maggie put her hand over the rift.

She didn't feel anything.

"See there," Maggie said. "Nothing happened."

"That's not very scientific," he said. "It could be radioactive."

"Then test it," Maggie said. "Test the air. Test the water. Do what you need to do. As far as we can tell, you all are standing around telling us to round up people while you're doing nothing. Why do you really want nonresidents all in one place?"

Shaw shrugged. "I told you. We want to figure out a way to get them home."

"You think one of them is a terrorist?"

"It could be," he said. "Or one of the residents is a terrorist. In either case, we want to know where everyone is." He looked down at his clipboard. "I see you haven't called in yet. Who's staying at your place?"

"Just me and the coyotes," Maggie said.

"Jack Coyote, you mean," Shaw said.

Maggie stared at him.

"This is scary ass stuff," Maggie said. "Do you understand that? Fix the damn road and get your nose out of our business.”

She got on her bike and started to pedal away. She wasn't quite sure why she was so angry. But something was not right. How many times was she going to say that before she believed it?

She stopped and turned around.

“Why don't the cars work on our side?” she asked.

Shaw said, “We have no idea.”

This time she believed he was telling the truth.

NEXT

Maggie stopped at Nina and John's house, but no one was home. Either that or they weren't answering the door. Maggie kept going until she got to Ricardo and Lisa's house. When she knocked, Lisa shouted for her to come in. Maggie opened the door and stepped inside. She smelled sugar. Or fruit.

She followed the sound of voices. She passed through the living room. The television was on the public access station. Maggie stopped and looked at it. "Stay tuned for important information about the Freeman Rift."

"The Freeman Rift," Maggie said. "They've already got a name for it. Probably have theme music, too."

"Maggie? Get your ass back here." Lisa's voice.

Maggie went into the kitchen. Steam rose from a pot on the stove. At the long wooden table, Ricardo and Alicia were spooning blueberries into glass jars. Lisa leaned against the counter and watched the pot.

"What's going on here?" Maggie said.

"We figure the electricity will go out next," Lisa said. "We've got a generator for a while, but eventually." She shrugged. "So we're thawing what we've got in the freezer and canning it. I meant to do this months ago, but I got behind this year."

"We'll have lots of blueberry jam for the end of the world," Ricardo said.

"Hey, when we're starving, you'll be happy for these blueberries," Lisa said. "I already canned lots of beans last summer. We will do good."

"So you don't believe this will end in a day or two?" Maggie asked.

Lisa shook her head. "They said they would drop us supplies, but they haven't done anything."

"The government used to own this land," Ricardo said. "Long time ago. I bet something in the fine print when we bought our places says they have a right to do experiments on us. That's probably what's happening right now. That's why they have to get all the nonresidents out. They never agreed to nothing like this."

Alicia kept spooning the blueberry mixture into the jars. She seemed unfazed by the talk.

"You believe this, Lisa?" Maggie asked.

"I believe we have to eat no matter what's happening," she said. "It doesn't look like they're fixing the road or coming over the rift so we need to take care of ourselves."

"Wouldn't it be better if we pooled our resources?" Maggie asked.

"That's what I was trying to do at the meeting last night," Lisa said. "People came for the party, but they didn't leave organized. We waste less if we eat and work together."

"I think that's true," Maggie said. "I don't have a lot to offer, food-wise though. I've got bags of beans, some rice, oats. Some fresh produce since I'd just been to the grocery store. My garden did not do well this year."

"For someone who talks with the plants," Ricardo said, "you have the worst luck with growing vegetables."

Maggie couldn't argue with that.

"I've talked to Nina and John," Lisa said. "They're in. They've got a freezer full of food and some dry goods."

"I can talk to Joanna," Maggie said. "But if I come, I'll probably bring Jack, Lisa, and I know you're not fond of him."

"As long as he isn't mooching off me, I don't care."

"Essentially he'll be mooching off all of us," Maggie said.

Lisa made a noise. "He can cook, I'll give him that."

"And there's one other thing," Maggie said, "but you can't tell anyone."

Lisa stood up straight. Her eyes brightened. Maggie laughed.

"No, really, you can't tell anyone," Maggie said. "You have to all promise me."

Lisa crossed her arms. "All right, all right. Alicia, Ricardo, keep your mouths shut about this."

"Oh yeah, Mom, we're the ones who can't keep a secret."

"Hush," Lisa said. "If I promise, I promise."

"Last night some strange things happened in the wash," Maggie said. She pulled out a chair and sat at the table.

"Yeah," Ricardo said. "It was a weird night. We wondered if someone put something in the salsa."

"The details aren't important, but Jack and I found this guy wandering in the wash. He's a little different. Doesn't seem to quite belong here. He calls himself Anders."

"I don't understand why that's a big secret," Lisa said. "So you've picked up another guy in the wash. Isn't that your specialty?" She winked.

Maggie shook her head. "They're asking that all non-residents meet over in some house on Broadway. They want to take them across the rift, they say. I think they may be looking for someone in particular."

"And you think they're looking for this man you found?" Ricardo asked.

"Shaw said there might be a terrorist," Maggie said.

"Is this new friend of yours a terrorist?" Lisa asked.

Maggie shook her head.

"How do you know?"

"The same way I know you're not a terrorist."

"But you've known me for a decade," Lisa said. "Besides, you don't really know."

"Lisa, I can't have this kind of discussion right now," Maggie said. "It's making my head hurt. He is not a terrorist. Wait until you meet him. But I don't think he should end up in the hands of the government."

"Why are you sounding so paranoid about the government all of a sudden?" Lisa asked.

"I'm not paranoid about the government per se," Maggie said. "I just think everything that has happened in the last couple of days has been very very very weird, as Jack's grandpa used to say."

The three of them looked at her. "Huh?"

"Nothing," Maggie said. "How about this? You meet him and decide. If we're going to do this resource and meal sharing, when do we start? And where do we bring the supplies?"

Lisa left the room and returned a moment later with a sheet of paper.

"I've got it all organized," she said as she dropped the paper in front of Maggie. "For now, we'll do lunch and dinner together. If you include your Anders character, that's nine of us. We'll take turns cooking and cleaning. Once we have a list of supplies, we'll sit down and figure out the menus."

Maggie glanced up at Lisa when she spotted her own name written down to cook a meal.

"Don't give me that look," Lisa said. "This will give you a chance to hone your cooking abilities."

"I get by just fine on my cooking," Maggie said. "And I can clean up better than anyone, I bet."

"Shared duties," Lisa said. "Isn't that what you do in communities? You're always the one talking about community. Here's your opportunity."

"And it's just us?" Maggie said. "No one else in the 'hood wants to join in? What about Bill and Tilly?"

"I phoned but Bill said they're doing just fine. Besides, do you want Bill to see Anders? Or see Jack for that matter. He'd turn them both in in a flat New York minute."

"What does that mean?" Alicia asked. "Is a New York minute different from a Tucson minute?"

"It's colder," Lisa said. "For the first dinner tonight, we'll make it here. Send Jack over to help."

"Mom, you should be nicer to Jack," Alicia said. "He's not your slave."

"He's my slave as long as he's in my kitchen," Lisa said.

"I love your community spirit," Ricardo said.

"Got that right," Lisa said.

Maggie pushed away from the table. "Oh, forgot to tell you. Joan Doud had Gabriel put up a fence across the wash."

Lisa and Ricardo looked at one another.

"No," Lisa said.

"Yep. Said it was her land and she didn't want trespassers."

"But I ride Jekyll through the wash all of the time," Alicia said, "to get to the park. Much safer than going down Speedway. I'm going to go talk to her."

"Let's wait," Ricardo said, "until all of this calms down. For now you can ride on Speedway. There aren't any cars on the roads now anyway."

Maggie picked up the paper with the schedule on it. "I'll see you tonight for dinner."

When Maggie got back to her house, Joanna, Jack, and Anders were sitting on the bunkhouse porch watching a raven pick at the dirt a few yards from them. Anders stood again when he saw Maggie. Jack did the same a second later.

"Why do you guys keep standing up?" Maggie asked. "This is America, remember? We don't have royalty."

Anders smiled at her. Maggie couldn't help but smile back. He had the most beautiful green eyes.

Maggie sat next to Joanna.

"They don't stand up for me," Joanna said. "That's for sure. So what's the buzz?"

"You first," Maggie said.

"Nothing new," Joanna said. "All of my clients—and

yours—were from the other side of the rift, so no one's coming. Nothing much to do today. Alex doesn't know anything new."

"I talked to that Shaw guy," Maggie said. "I think he's lying to us."

Anders and the crow gazed at one another. Anders nodded and smiled. The crow shook its head and pecked at the dirt again.

Jack looked over Anders's head at Maggie and made a kind of "what the hell?" face.

"Shaw knows about you, Jack," Maggie said, "but he doesn't know about Anders."

Anders looked at her and then back at the crow.

Maggie said, "They want all the nonresidents in one place because they think the rift may have been caused by a terrorist attack."

"Terrorist attack?" Jack said. "Where would they get a notion like that?"

Anders looked at Jack. "A notion," he said, as though the word were new to him. He nodded. "Potion, motion, lotion, emotion, locomotion. Notion. Comes from the word 'idea.'"

"He's been doing that all day," Jack said.

"Is English not your first language?" Maggie asked.

"I speak English," Anders said.

"Yes, I know, but—never mind," Maggie said. "I don't think we should let anyone take Anders any-where."

"I cannot leave this place," he said.

"I won't tell anyone he's here," Joanna said, "and if he stays here, chances are no one will see him."

Maggie took the meal schedule from her back pocket and unfolded it.

"We've decided to pool our resources," Maggie said, "in case this lasts for a while. So far it's just a few of us, but I thought you all would want to be a part of it. If so, we'll share food and cooking duties. Jack, you're supposed to go early and help Lisa with the cooking."

"I am willing and ready to do my duty to God and my country," Jack said. "Actually, I'm willing and ready to do my duty to Mags and this little stretch of dirt I've called home these last few weeks."

Joanna looked at the schedule. "Sure, sounds good."

"I need to see if there's anything in my garden I can salvage," Maggie said, "since fresh produce is going to be the first thing that runs out."

"I'll go home and feed the horses and cat," Joanna said. "I'll see you all later at Lisa and Ricardo's place."

Joanna left, and Jack and Anders followed Maggie out to the west corral which she had turned into a garden. Ricardo had helped her create the wall that went around it to keep out the javelinas and rabbits. She opened the gate and went through it. She stood looking at the ground with her hands on her hips. She shook her head.

"Man, this is pathetic."

Anders walked past her and bent over one of the kale bunches. He put his hand on a withered leaf. Then he looked over at her. "They are barely alive."

Maggie bit her lip as a pang of guilt shot through her.

"I know," Maggie said. "I don't know what happens. I just forget. Fortunately, I've got a grey water system set up and that at least helps the bushes."

"Looks like this needs a bit of tending," Jack said. "Not all is lost, Mags. Not all is lost."

"Coyote Jack and I can make it well," Anders said.

Maggie looked at Jack. "Wouldn't hurt to try," he said.

"All right," Maggie said. "I want to go check on Tilly and see what's happening with the nonresident house. I'll meet you two at dinner. Don't let anyone but John, Nina, or Ricardo's family see Anders."

Anders stood. "You want me to disappear? I can do that."

Maggie smiled. "At least disappear when strangers are around. I think you'll be safer that way."

Anders squatted next to the plants again.

"I'll be right back, Andy," Jack said. He followed Maggie out of the garden. She shut the gate behind them.

"Um, Mags, I don't understand about Anders," he said. "Why do you think he's in trouble? Why don't you want people to know about him?"

"I don't know," she said. "I just feel protective of him. He seems so lost and innocent."

"You think he's retarded?" Jack said. "I heard there were a few group homes around here."

"I don't think they use that word any more," Maggie said. "But that's a good point. There are group homes around here. I can't remember if they're on this side or the other side of the rift. I'll have to ask Lisa later."

"I know what you're thinking," Jack said. "You're thinking he is one of those aliens. His ship crashed or something and caused all of this and you don't want them catching him and poking and prodding him and slicing him up into little bits to study."

"Ew," Maggie said. "I hope they wouldn't do that.

But no, I don't think he's from another planet. We'll figure this out later. Thanks, Jack."

Jack looked like he wanted to say more, but he didn't. He went back to the garden. Maggie ducked into Desert Bloomers and phoned Alexandria.

"Hey, Alex," Maggie said. "It's Maggie. How are you doing? Your gal sure misses you."

"I'm good, Maggie," Alex said. "Although this situation gets weirder and weirder."

"I need to ask you a favor," Maggie said. "I don't know how to get this info, particularly since the internet doesn't work here, but maybe you can figure it out. I'd like to find out if there are any adult group homes on this side of the rift, or nearby, and if there are, I want to know if they've lost any residents."

In case anyone was eavesdropping on them, Maggie needed to come up with a cover story. "We just want to help out our neighbors in any way we can." A lousy cover story, but there it was.

"I'll find out what I can," Alex said. "Joanna there?"

"She went home to feed the animals," Maggie said, "but later we'll be at Lisa and Ricardo's house. We've formed a little cooperative."

"What are you calling it? The Desert Late Bloomers?"

Maggie laughed.

"Hey, I did learn something since I talked to Joanna last," Alex said. "They've got a map of the rift now. It's not a straight line. It curves. In the north it goes up to the Catalina Mountains. To the south, it curves east and goes right into the Rincons. So there's really no place to get around the rift, from your perspective. You've got mountains on one side of you and the rift on all the other sides."

"Wow," Maggie said. "That really does cut us off from everything, except overhead. I haven't seen anything overhead, come to think of it."

"They've restricted the airspace over that area," Alexandria said.

"You should hear the rumors," Maggie said. "Latest one is that it was a terrorist bomb."

"They are going to send drones over to test the air," Alexandria said.

"But it's been almost two days," Maggie said. "Wouldn't we already be sick?"

"Depends upon what it was," Alexandria said. "If it was something radioactive, it might take a while."

"Shit," Maggie said. "You don't think any of that is true, do you?"

"No, no," Alexandria said. "I'm sure everyone is fine. I'll let you know if I find anything out about the group homes."

"Thanks."

Maggie and Alex said good-bye, and Maggie hung up the phone. She felt butterflies in her stomach. She had assumed all the paranoia was unfounded: The rift was caused by an earthquake. Period. Now she wasn't sure. Maybe the reason she hadn't been able to connect with the plants and animals in the wash and desert was because something was interfering.

Like radiation?

"Shit. Fuck. Piss." She glanced at the crystals, rocks, and plants around the shop. She chuckled. "Excuse my French."

NEXT

Maggie hurried out of the shop, stepped into the wash, then headed south. It was too sandy to ride her bike, so she had to count on her feet to get her from here to there. She couldn't have ridden her bike in the wash anyway, she suddenly remembered, because of that damned fence. That stupid fence. Everything felt different. Stifled. As if the flow of the wash had been altered—or damned. Dammed? As she had the thought, she saw three strands of barbed wire going from one side of the wash to the other. In the middle was a big black sign with orange lettering: PRIVATE PROPERTY NO TRESPASSING.

Maggie growled and ducked under the fence and kept walking. The mesquite trees, agave plants, prickly pear pads, even the sparkly sand—except for the tractor tracks in the dirt—all looked the same. But it felt different. Anger welled up inside of Maggie. She let it out in a howl.

In the distance, another coyote answered her.

Further down, in the widest part of the dry river that was the wash, Maggie saw a metal post with a "no trespassing" sign strung onto it.

"You can't put a no trespassing sign in a river!" Maggie shouted.

Only the desert silence answered her.

She came out of the wash on to Fifth Street. She looked up and down the dirt road. The police cars were still down by the rift. She turned the other way and headed for Bill and Tilly's place.

A moment after she pushed the buzzer, Bill and Tilly's gate creaked open.

She saw Bill in the barn, so she went over to say hello.

"How's Tilly?" Maggie asked.

Bill nodded. "She's good." He always said that, no matter how Tilly was feeling. "I've got an idea on how to get her out of here."

"Bill, she doesn't want to got out of here," Maggie said.

"That's just because of you and Joanna feeding her all that bull crap about natural healing," he said.

"Joanna and I don't feed her anything except herbs and flower essences," Maggie said. "We've never discouraged her from getting conventional treatments."

Bill waved a hand in dismissal. They had had this exchange many times before.

"None of that matters," he said. "They've got all those tourists—what they're calling nonresidents—in that house on Broadway. I know they're going to take them across to the other side. We could take Tilly there, tell them she's a tourist. Off she'll go. My sister can pick her up on the other side!"

"What's this 'we', paleface?" I said. "Tilly will not go along with this."

He shrugged. "She might," he said. "If I get her drunk enough."

Maggie disagreed with Bill about nearly everything political, spiritual, and economic, but she knew he would never do anything to deliberately harm Tilly, including getting her drunk.

"She's got a doctor's appointment in a few days," he said, "and I want her to keep it."

"I know, Bill," she said. "Look, I've been hearing some wild rumors. I'm trying to figure out a way to disprove some of them before people start panicking."

"If you're talking about the rumor that I will shoot to kill anyone who comes onto my property, you can tell them that is not a goddamn rumor."

"Settle down, cowboy," Maggie said. "I'm talking about the rumors of radiation, alien invasion, all that. In all your survivalist gear, do you have anything that can detect radiation?"

"You mean like a Geiger counter?" he asked. "Sure. That's amateur stuff. I already checked. Went all over the neighborhood. Nothing. Was some down by the rift. Not sure if that happens during earthquakes or not. Can't get anything on the internets."

"Thanks, Bill," Maggie said. "That's actually very reassuring."

"Geiger counter can't detect the thousands of other things that could be floating around in our air or water though," Bill said. "So don't be reassured. Go on and see Tilly. But don't fill her head with any nonsense."

"That's your job, eh?" Maggie said.

"Got that right."

Maggie went into the house. She found Tilly in the living room. The television was on, tuned to the soundless public access channel. On screen was the message: "Please stay tuned for important information about the Freeman Rift."

"I'm not watching it," Tilly said. "I just have it on for company."

Maggie laughed and sat next to Tilly on the couch. "Doesn't look like it's very good company. How you doing?" Maggie looked at her. She seemed a bit paler than she had yesterday.

"I'm fine," Tilly said. "I had another dream last night. Queen Anne's Lace came and told me I should go."

"Go where?"

Tilly smiled. "I have no idea. I asked her if she meant I was going to die. She said I should go to the other side."

"Really? What do you think that meant?"

"It could mean I'm dying, but it could mean something else."

"Could it mean you need to go to the other side of the rift?" Maggie asked.

Tilly looked at her. "I hadn't thought of that."

"You know, Bill has this crazy scheme about getting you to the other side of the rift," Maggie said. "He wants you to pretend you're a tourist and go to that house on Broadway."

Tilly laughed. "That's silly. My driver's license says I live here."

"You wouldn't have to take your driver's license," Maggie said, "or you could say you had recently moved and hadn't gotten it changed yet."

"But why would I want to go?" Tilly said. "I'm perfectly fine here."

"I don't know," Maggie said. "I was just wondering if that's what your dream meant."

Maggie took Tilly's pulses. "Did you sleep much last night?"

"Not a lot," Tilly said. "Did you see that moon? And I haven't been hungry today."

"You know, Tilly, I understand not wanting to go to more doctors," Maggie said, "or to do more aggressive therapy. But sometimes simple things can extend our lives. You've been a bit rundown lately. Maybe the doctor can figure out why."

"The why is that I'm dying," Tilly said. "That'll run you down in no time."

Maggie laughed. "I hear you, Tilly. A bunch of us are joining forces, so to speak, in case we're stuck here for a while, sharing food and other supplies. We're going to take turns cooking. Would you and Bill like to be a part of it?"

"That's kind of you to offer, Maggie," Tilly said, "but Bill would never go for it, and truth to tell, I'm not sure I'm up to being around a bunch of people."

"Might do you some good to have more company," Maggie said.

"Right now I'm the only company I want," Tilly said. "Except for Bill and the wild creatures. And you, of course."

Maggie smiled. "Just let me know if you change your mind, or even if you just want me to bring you some meals."

"I sure will," she said.

Bill called out to Maggie as she walked down the drive past the barn.

"Hey, Maggie, look what just wandered into my corral."

Maggie followed Bill through the barn and out the back. In the bright winter sunlight, a tall blue-black horse stood in Bill and Tilly's south corral, away from the other horses. The horse looked directly at Bill and Maggie. Maggie knew him. She had seen him in the wash last night, only he had been a lighter blue. Now he was the blue-black color of a crow. His mane and tail were long and wavy. His eyes were golden. And then brown.

He reared and whinnied. Then he ran to the end of the corral and leaped over the fence.

Maggie and Bill stood silently next to one another for a few moments.

"I wish Tilly could have seen him," Bill said. "Now that was a horse."

"I have a feeling he'll be back," Maggie said.

Maggie left Bill and Tilly's and walked a couple of blocks until she got to Broadway. She looked east—toward the park and the Rincons. Dead cars still lined the park fence. She looked west and saw the rift and several police cars with their lights flashing. She wondered why they didn't turn those off. She also saw people milling around a house near the rift. She thought about going down there, but it was almost dinner time. She started to walk back toward home but instead of turning, she continued walking down Broadway to the park.

She stood on the inconspicuous entrance to the park—just an opening in the fence with a sign warning hikers about mountain lions and killer bees. She whispered a blessing, as she always did before entering. "I ask permission to enter. I intend no harm, may no harm come to me." Then she stepped over the threshold. She wondered how many people noticed thresholds. Walking into a building. Running into a park. Slip-sliding into a wash.

Maggie always sensed a difference, a fluttering, a slight disturbance like when a pebble is dropped into a pool of water. And today she noticed a shift in the energy from outside the park to the inside of the park. She stood on the dirt path and looked around at the saguaros, various prickly pear bushes, teddy bear cholla, mesquite and paloverde trees. Pebbles and shards of mica on the path glittered in the light from the sun that was sinking toward the west now. Everything was still. Silent.

But something was different. Maggie was not quite certain what. She was holding her breath, she realized. So she let it out and breathed deeply. She walked over to a saguaro. One of its limbs had twisted earthward.

"Hello, Old One," Maggie said. "What's going on?" She carefully reached out and touched the downy top of the limb, maneuvering her finger between the thorns. It felt like rabbit's fur. Or cotton. That was it. Like cotton. She remembered the first time she had touched this part of a saguaro and how surprised she had been to find this softness amidst all the thorns. She wished she could embrace a saguaro the way Anders had. All in. Not worried for a moment about getting hurt. Maybe because he couldn't get hurt. Maybe because whatever he was, he could not be hurt by a saguaro cactus.

Maggie loved saguaro medicine. It was strengthening. Gave people backbone. Helped them do what they needed to do.

Maggie was not sure what she needed to do in this situation. What could she do? She couldn't fix the rift.

Could she?

She heard the sound of wings beating in the dry air. She looked up as a raven flew overhead.

Time to go to Ricardo's place.

Everyone was already at the house when Maggie arrived, eight of them sitting around Lisa and Ricardo's long wooden kitchen table. Anders was talking and everyone was listening in rapt attention, even Lisa. John and Nina stared at Anders, open-mouthed.

"Hello," Maggie said.

"And that was that," Anders said. He smiled and stood. "Hello, Miss Maggie."

"He was telling us about the conversation he heard between two crows in the corral today," Alicia said. "I've always wondered if they were gossips, and now I know they are."

Jack pushed away from the table and went to the stove. "I just wonder if it's polite to eavesdrop on crows. Doesn't seem quite neighborly."

"They should keep their voices down if they don't wish to be overheard," Ricardo said.

Maggie looked at Lisa. She smiled and shrugged. Jack stirred the contents of two pots on the stove. Anders offered Maggie his chair. He reached for her hand. Without thinking, Maggie put her hand in his. She felt a slight spark of static electricity again.

"See how we connect," Anders whispered.

Maggie smiled. She looked around, but no one was paying any attention to them. She sat in Anders's chair and he sat beside her.

"Where you been?" Lisa asked. Lisa and Joanna began setting the table. Ricardo drained water from the fettuccine pasta.

"I went to see Tilly and Bill," Maggie said. "Bill says he's going to take Tilly to the Broadway house in hopes of getting her to the other side? She's got a doctor's appointment he doesn't want her to miss. I'm starting to believe it might not be a bad idea. I also talked to Alexandria. Did she tell you, Joanna?"

Joanna nodded. "Yep, she just called here. Said there are no missing residents of any adult homes." She glanced at Anders. "So he's not from there."

Ricardo dropped the pasta into a bowl and took it to Jack. Jack poured marinara sauce over it, and then Ricardo tossed the sauce and the pasta. Alicia brought a salad to the table. Ricardo set the pasta dish on the table. Then everyone sat.

"Thank you all for coming and sharing this meal," Lisa said. "We thank the plants that provided us with this food, we thank the people who harvested these plants, and we thank the cooks who put together this food."

Everyone nodded.

"Dig in," Lisa said.

They began passing dishes around.

"Why were you asking about adult homes?" John asked.

Maggie glanced at Anders.

"You thought he was from one of those homes?" Nina asked. "Not really? He's brilliant. He couldn't be from there. Anders, tell her. You're from one of the stars, aren't you?"

"Geez Louise, Nina," Lisa said. "You can't believe that nonsense?"

"Look at him," Nina said. "Doesn't he look like he's from another world?"

"No," Lisa said. "Maybe from another county."

Maggie glanced at Anders. He seemed oblivious to the discussion. He piled spaghetti and salad on his plate so that it was nearly overflowing.

"Are you hungry, Anders?" Jack asked. "I've been feeding him all day. I think he's got a hollow leg or something."

"Everything tastes so good," Anders said. "You are all so generous."

"Anders," Maggie said, "can you tell us where you're from?"

"I am from here," Anders said.

"You live in this neighborhood?" Ricardo asked. "I've never seen you before."

"I have never seen you before either," Anders said.

"Okay," Maggie said. "So we can all relax. He's a resident."

"I wasn't unrelaxed," Lisa said. "But I agree that we don't need to go advertising that he's with us, if you know what I mean."

"You don't want us to tell Mr. Shaw," Alicia said, "or those people who keep calling and asking who's staying at our house."

"What is that all about anyway?" Joanna asked. "I keep getting messages from them, but when I try to call the number they left, it's always busy."

"I'm not calling them back," Maggie said. "If they want to know who's in my house they can come knock on my door."

"Why don't you want them to know?" Alicia asked. "Maybe it's like the census."

"The census is anonymous," Lisa said. "They don't really know who we are with that. I'm not normally paranoid—"

Maggie almost spit out her food.

"You are abnormally paranoid!" Maggie said.

"Okay," Lisa said. "So I am paranoid. But I don't worry about the census. And I don't worry about lots of things. This, however, is very strange."

"Did I tell you when I spoke to Shaw he knew Jack was staying at my place?" Maggie asked. "Now how the hell could he know that?"

Jack held up a hand. "I didn't tell him. I have not talked to anyone from the government."

"I've talked to the people who are calling," Nina said. "They seem really nice. I told them everything I know about people in the neighborhood. They said they needed to know to get us food and supplies."

"Did you tell them Jack was staying with me?" Maggie asked.

"I think I may have," Nina said. "I didn't know it was a secret."

John patted her hand.

"It's not a secret," Maggie said. "But Anders is a secret. Don't tell anyone, please."

"I am a secret," Anders said. "What is a secret? From 'separate,' and 'to set apart.' I don't wish to be separate."

"You won't be separate," Maggie said. "You'll be with us."

"I know what's happening is upsetting and strange," Joanna said, "but I don't understand this sudden mistrust of the government. The government hasn't done anything."

"Exactly," Maggie said. "Doesn't it seem strange to you that they haven't done *anything?* Why aren't they fixing the road? Why won't they let us try to get to the other side?"

"I don't know," Joanna said. "Has anyone actually tried to get to the other side. I've heard it's a little narrower in some areas. A horse could probably jump it."

"They could build a temporary bridge in no time," Ricardo said. "Put down a couple pieces of wood and there you are."

"Why do you want to go to the other side?" Alicia asked. "We've got plenty here."

"You just don't want to go back to school," Lisa said.

Alicia shrugged. "I like that everyone's around. And it seems quieter."

"Are you sure you're a teenager?" John asked. "Shouldn't you want things bigger and better, louder and louder?"

"Leave her alone and eat," Lisa said. "I hope you all brought a list of supplies so we can sit down and create some menus for the coming days."

"Tomorrow I will go around the neighborhood and see if anyone has tried crossing over," Ricardo said. "Jack, you wanna come?"

Jack nodded.

"Alexandria has contacted our state and federal reps," Joanna said. "They say they're doing whatever they can to fix this. Although I don't know what they can do."

"They can get someone out here to fix the damn roads," Maggie said. "Or at least build new ones."

"Don't you like the quiet, Maggie?" Alicia asked.

"So far, darlin', I haven't noticed a lot of quiet,"

Maggie said. "Feels like I've been running for days, even though it's only been a couple of days and I slept half of one of those days away."

"I bet in the morning it'll all be different," Joanna said. "They'll fix the road and all will return to normal. I could use some normal. Feels like Alex and I have been apart forever."

"It is all different," Anders said, looking up from his plate of food for the first time. "It will never be the same again."

NEXT

Maggie couldn't sleep. She rarely had trouble sleeping, but this night she tossed and turned. She kept thinking she heard Irving bark. She'd get up and open the front door and listen. Nothing. Desert silence.

She noticed the light on in the bunkhouse. She put on her slippers and walked out to the barn. She started to knock on Jack's door. But she stopped and listened.

She heard weeping.

Then swearing. Jack's voice.

Then weeping. Jack weeping.

She wondered if she should ask if he needed help. Ask if he needed something.

But it wasn't any of her business.

Was he struggling not to drink?

Was he struggling with the grief Maggie had felt when she touched him?

What could she possibly say to him? She wouldn't know how to comfort him.

She did not really understand men. If she thought about it, she didn't actually understand women either. But she felt comfortable asking them to tell her what they needed. She felt comfortable reaching out to them.

Men seemed like completely different creatures. She supposed she hadn't taken enough time and effort during her lifetime to understand them. As if "them" could be understood. She worked with plants, she worked with animals, she worked with the elements. She had a level of knowledge and comfort with them.

Why not with men?

She knew how to have sex with them. She did not know how to talk with them.

She turned and hurried away from the barn.

"You are a coward, Maggie girl," she whispered as she went back toward the house. She glanced up at the moon. The moonlight made the whole desert look milky. She looked back at the barn. She hoped Jack felt better soon and Anders slept well.

Maggie awakened to the sound of Irving barking. She opened her eyes and listened and realized someone was pounding on her front door again. She sat up, pulled on her jeans, and threw on a shirt over her camisole as she hurried to the door.

"Who is it?" she called.

"Mags, there's a helicopter overhead. Looks like a big one." Jack's voice.

She opened the door.

She could hear the helicopter in the near distance. She stepped outside and looked up. Nothing but the night sky.

"I think it's over on Broadway," he said.

"We could never get there fast enough on foot," she said.

Maggie ran back into the house, picked up her phone, and called Ricardo's land line. Jack followed her inside.

"Better be the end of the world." Lisa's voice.

"There's a helicopter," Maggie said. "On Broadway, I think. Can you have Ricardo bring his truck and drive us over? We'll meet him on Speedway."

"Done."

Maggie hung up. Jack and Maggie went back outside, then hurried down the drive.

"Is Anders still asleep?" Maggie asked.

"I think so," Jack said. "His door was closed."

They got to Speedway just as Ricardo pulled up. Lisa and Alicia were in the front. Jack and Maggie jumped in the back. The truck sped forward, knocking Maggie into Jack. She could still hear the whoop-whoop-whoop of the helicopter. Maggie pushed herself off of Jack.

"Fine by me if you stay there," Jack said. "Felt downright cozy."

Maggie didn't say anything. She figured she'd let Jack do his version of flirting, even though they'd had that little talk about just being friends. Maybe he needed a flirtation after bawling his eyes out earlier.

The truck bounced down Aguila Street, kicking up dust as it went. Ricardo turned the truck down Broadway. Up ahead Maggie could see what looked like a military transport helicopter on the road.

Then, just like that, the helicopter rose up off the road. Ricardo didn't even slow the truck down. The wind from the helicopter blades whipped Maggie's hair into her face. She couldn't see for a moment. But then she saw someone standing near the helicopter, fists raised to the sky, yelling.

It was Bill.

The chopper moved off to the west, over the rift and away from them. Ricardo stopped the truck. Maggie hopped out and tried to watch the helicopter, but it quickly disappeared into the night.

She ran over to Bill.

"Goddamn mother fuckers," he yelled. "You'll be sorry."

"Bill! What's happened?"

He kept yelling. He didn't seem to notice her.

"Bill!" She grabbed his arm.

He looked at her, then jerked away.

"They came for the others," he said, "but they wouldn't take Tilly. She wasn't on their list. So they wouldn't take her. I swear if I'd had my gun I would have killed them all."

"Where is Tilly?" Maggie asked.

"She's inside," he said.

Maggie hurried down the drive and went inside the strange house. All the lights were on, and Tilly sat on a chair at the kitchen table. Her face looked flushed. She smiled when she saw Maggie.

"Now that was quite an adventure!" Tilly said.

"Are you all right?" Maggie asked.

"I am," she said. "We rode over on the horses. Haven't ridden at night in ages. Actually, I don't know that I've ever ridden at night. The horses were absolute dears, though. I felt like I was on the ride of a lifetime. Once we were here, I just tried to blend in with everyone else. And then the helicopter came. Bill said it would be tonight and he was right. Some government guy got off. He was dressed in a biohazard suit. Checked everyone off a list. Only had to make one trip. Got everyone on that big old thing. But they wouldn't take me. Bill pleaded with them. And then he got angry. I was afraid he was going to get shot. They had guns."

Maggie sighed. "I'm sorry, Tilly."

"That's that," she said. "I am tired though. Not sure I can go back on the horses."

"Ricardo's got his pickup," Maggie said. "He'll take you home."

Lisa came into the house.

"Tilly, my girl, that was a great escape plan," Lisa said. "Too bad it didn't work. At least we know now it's horseshit when they say it's dangerous to go over the rift."

Tilly slowly got up. "I wonder why this is happening to us now," Tilly said. "It seems like such a strange thing." Maggie and Lisa got on either side of Tilly and she leaned on them as they left the kitchen.

"We just happened to be on the wrong side of the line," Lisa said.

"Maybe not," Tilly said. "Just think of all the things we don't have to deal with over here. It's just us, the desert, and the mountains."

"Yeah, I don't know if we're going to feel like that if we run out of food."

Maggie gave Lisa a look.

"Not that that's going to happen," Lisa said. "It's going to be over soon, and we'll have this little adventure to talk about for a long time."

Bill and Tilly got into the passenger side of the truck, next to Ricardo, after they convinced Bill not to trash the Broadway house as an act of revenge against whomever it was who wouldn't take Tilly. None of the four in the back of the truck said anything to one another as they drove to the Boyle house. Maggie thought about how quickly things had changed—how quickly they had dropped into stress mode once their daily routines were disrupted.

Jack and Maggie walked back to her house from Speedway.

"Can I come in for a cup of coffee or something?" Jack asked.

"Don't you want to try to sleep?"

Jack shook his head. "I'd prefer some company."

Maggie opened her front door, switched on the lights, and walked inside. Jack followed and closed the door behind him.

"I don't have any coffee," Maggie said. "Suppose I should for company but I never got in the habit, and I don't have much company. I keep tea for Joanna, though. You're welcome to that."

"Sure," he said.

She went to the kitchen.

"Can I help?" he asked.

"No," Maggie said. "Not this time. Just don't get used to me waiting on you. It ain't going to be a routine thing."

"Never crossed my mind," Jack said. He pulled out a chair from the kitchen table and sat in it.

"You have a bad night, Jack?" Maggie asked. It wasn't any of her business, but she asked it anyway. If she had overheard Joanna crying, she would have asked her what was up.

"Aw, it's nuthin' you need to worry your magnificent self over," he said.

 KIM ANTIEAU

Maggie put water in the kettle and then set it on the stove and turned the burner on. She got two cups out of the cupboard, along with a box of herbal and black teas. She put them all on the table, then pulled out a chair across from Jack.

"I'm not worried," she said. "It's just what I do."

"Take care of people?" he said. "You do a fine job of it, too."

He looked at her and smiled.

"What?" she said.

"I was wondering if you actually have relationships with people," Jack said, "or are you trying to fix them? You always seem on the edges of things even when you're in the middle of the action."

"Why, Coyote Jack, I wouldn't expect to hear something like that from you. That could be insightful, if it were true."

"I'm just making an observation," he said. "It seems to me you are always trying to fix things. Heal people. I'm wondering if that leaves much time for friendships and lovin' and whatnot. I'm just saying, Mags. It was not meant as any kind of criticism. Hell, how could I criticize? I'm not much for relationships myself. I'd like one but I'm not very good at it."

"Maybe that's because you're so often on the make," Maggie said. "Sometimes it's difficult to see through to your true heart when you're doing that. You remind me of this ol' coyote I see most every day in the wash. He's always on the lookout for some new female coyote. But he's always alone. Alone with his tongue hanging out."

Jack laughed. "I don't believe my tongue is ever hanging out."

"In fact, I haven't seen Old Brandy since you arrived," Maggie said. "Maybe he shape-changed into you."

"Just to get to you?" Jack asked. "I bet that old coyote has been lusting after you all these years. That's what I think."

"Then he mistook himself," Maggie said.

Jack smiled, but he didn't seem to mean it. He looked tired again. Maggie kind of liked his bravado. It was irritating but relaxing. She didn't have to worry about trying to fix him.

Worry. There was that word again. Maybe she did worry about everyone.

The kettle whistled. Jack stood up and got the kettle and poured water into their cups. He set the kettle back on the stove and sat down again. He picked a tea bag from the box and dropped it into his cup.

"You want one?" he asked.

She shook her head. "I drink hot water," she said. "I call it Zen tea."

He laughed. "I like that."

Maggie smiled. "You know, I tell waiters and waitresses all the time when I order hot water than it's really Zen tea, and no one ever gets it. I think you're the first."

"I do have a good sense of humor," Jack said. "Tonight though, I was wanting a drink more than almost anything. I thought about knocking on your door and seeing if you wanted company, but I felt too raw, you know? Like I might spill my guts and tell you everything about my life. And who wants to hear that? I don't even want to hear that. What matters is the here and now. I'm here now with you."

"Have you tried AA?" Maggie asked.

"I have," he said, "and it helps, even though I don't believe I am any kind of alcoholic. I only drink because I'm sad."

"Why do you think other people drink?"

He shrugged. "I don't much care why, I guess. Sometimes the sadness just feels so deep I cannot abide it. Do you ever feel sad?"

"I don't know," Maggie said. If she actually stopped to think about it, she was not certain what she felt. "When I was younger, I didn't want to have anything to do with mainstream culture. I didn't want the house in the suburbs, or the nine to five job, or the repressed angry husband or the two point five children. I wanted to do my own thing and live my own life. So here I am at the edge of the desert talking to plant spirits, rescuing who knows what from the wash, and keeping my neighbors from shooting at helicopters. Maybe that's a little too far from the mainstream."

Jack shook his head. "Ricardo thinks I get this way cuz of a woman. And it's true that I have had some recent heartbreak in that area, but I can see now that she was not the one for me. Mostly it's heartbreak when I look around and see all the isolation. People walking around talking on cell phones but not to each other. I see people in the park jogging with music going in one ear and a cell phone in the other and they are not even noticing what's around them. They wouldn't talk to a plant. Hell, they'd hardly talk to a person. The other day on the street downtown, I saw some man with a woman and a child and he was talking on the phone, wasn't paying any attention to the woman or the kid, and they all three looked so lonely and isolated."

"I'm pissed that they aren't fixing the road," Maggie said, "but I don't mind being on this side. On that side is a strip city. Look at Speedway and Broadway. Strip malls reaching out into the desert. Just glass and steel and plastic. Everything's on the move all the time. Those roads have become like the wash, I suppose, only they're filled with cars all the time instead of water."

"Humans are pack animals, but we aren't comfortable with our own kind," Jack said.

"Yeah, I liked being around Irving more than any other person," Maggie said. "I do miss him. Hey, when you first came here you kept asking if I was the one. What was that all about?"

"I told you," he said. "I thought you could make me a love potion."

"Ah yes," she said. "Who would be the lucky recipient of this love potion?"

"I thought you could give it to me and then I would attract some fine young thing."

"Young thing?"

"Just a figure of speech," Jack said. "I would be perfectly happy with some fine old thing."

"Jack!" Maggie said.

"I'm razzing you," he said. "I don't think of women as fine or young or old or, most especially, as things. I think of women as someone I can cuddle up to at night to take the blues away."

"I don't think a person can take your blues away," Maggie said.

"Then what will?"

Maggie shook her head. "Maybe if you felt good about yourself, if you felt at home, then the blues would dissipate."

"All sickness is homesickness," Jack said. "I read that somewhere once."

"I think it's the truth," Maggie said.

"I don't feel much at home anywhere," Jack said. "It's the wanderer in me."

"I thought wanderers felt at home everywhere," Maggie said.

Jack shrugged. "How about you? You feel at home in this old world?"

"A lot of the time I do. Especially if I don't think about it too much."

Jack laughed. "Isn't that the cure for most things ailing us?"

"Maybe." Maggie yawned. "I think this conversation got deeper than I wanted it to be in the middle of the night."

Jack drank the last of his tea.

"I appreciate the company," he said, "and am glad you jumped into the deep end with me. It's good for the soul."

"I suppose so," Maggie said.

He pushed away from the table, stood, then leaned over and kissed the top of Maggie's head.

"Good sleeps, darlin'," he said. "I'll see you in the morning."

"You, too, Jack."

She watched him leave. Then she got up and cleared the table. After, she locked the front door and went back to bed.

NEXT

NEXT

In the morning, no one answered when Maggie knocked on the Desert Bloomers door. She slowly opened it. The room was empty. Didn't look as though Anders had slept there. Either that or he had awakened very early, tidied up and then left.

Maggie went out to the garden. She opened the gate and stepped inside. Jack was bent over the plants with Anders beside him. Anders stood, walked over to her, and put his arms around her. Maggie felt herself sinking into him.

"I've missed you," Anders said. "I heard you had an adventure last night."

Anders released her and Maggie reluctantly moved away. She smiled at him. He was using more and bigger words, as though he was learning a new language and getting better at it every hour.

"An adventure?" Maggie said. She nodded to Jack.

"You mean the helicopter taking the nonresidents away?"

"I did not hear about that," Anders said. "I meant you and Jack had tea together."

Maggie laughed. Jack stood, leaned on his hoe, and grinned.

"I didn't tell him nothin', Mags," Jack said. "All your secrets are safe with me."

"Then I should have tea with Maggie," Anders said, "because her secrets would not be safe with me."

Anders walked through the open gate and left. Jack came over to Maggie. They watched Anders walk toward the barn.

"I don't think he slept in the shop," Jack said. "I didn't hear a thing all night. I wonder if he sleeps at all."

"Of course he sleeps," Maggie said. "Every human being needs to sleep."

Jack said. "Exactly."

"All right, every living being needs to sleep. And he's definitely living."

Maggie had to cancel her appointments for the day again. All of her clients were from the other side of the rift. She called each client. She worked with a couple of them over the phone. She told them where in town they could pick up her flower essences. She preferred in-person consultations, but she could continue doing phone consults for a while. Until they fixed the road.

Maggie sat in the chair outside of Desert Bloomers and wondered what she would do this day. Funny, she had not realized before that most of the people who came to see her were not from her own neighborhood.

She wondered why. Did that mean everyone who knew her thought her work was worthless?

She shook her head. Where had that come from? And why was she sitting here ruminating? She loved winters in the Sonoran Desert. She loved walking through the desert at all times of the day in the winter. It was a gift that she didn't have clients today. It was an unexpected vacation.

Joanna did not call or come over. All of Joanna's clients were from over the rift, too. Maybe she was doing phone consults from home.

Jack came by. "You look like you're up to no good. Come on, let's go for a walk."

"I don't want to leave Anders here alone," she said.

"He told me he was going to sleep," Jack said. "I guess he's still on alien time. You look like you're brewin' and stewin'. That's what I do before I start drinking. Let's go burn off some of that ruminatin'."

Maggie and Jack walked through the wash, heading toward Fifth Street. Maggie swore under her breath when she saw the fence. Jack held two strands of the wire open so she could get through, and then she did the same for him. At the end of the wash, they stepped out onto Fifth. Cop cars were still parked on the other side of the rift, only now their flashing lights were off.

Maggie and Jack headed east on Fifth. All looked quiet at Bill and Tilly's house. They turned right on Aguila. It was a gorgeous winter day: The sky was clear and blue, the air about 60 degrees. No wind. Yet no one out. No car, no horse, no pedestrian. No dog even barked.

They turned left on Broadway and walked until they got to the park entrance. Maggie asked permission to enter and said her blessings. Jack stood with his hands folded and his head down. Maggie could feel him relax as she whispered to the east and the air, the south and the fire, the west and the water, the north and the earth.

"We intend no harm," she said, "and wish to pass in peace and safety."

They stepped over the threshold and started down the south trail. Maggie noticed birds in the trees and cacti as they walked by: a phainopepla, cactus wren, mourning dove. They each watched Jack and Maggie as they walked by but none of them called out or alarmed on them. Everything seemed preternaturally quiet and still today.

Then Maggie began hearing a dull roar in the distance. She had heard it before.

Jack stopped and listened. "What is that?" he asked.

"I've never known," she said, "but I'm pretty sure it has something to do with the Air Force base. Sounds like jets revving their motors."

The noise got louder, faded, and then got louder again.

"It's like listening to a million leaf blowers."

"Yep, it's really spoiling a good walk," Maggie said.

"I wonder if they're gearing up for something," Jack said. "Like a bombing run."

"Maybe," Maggie said. "I hope not. I especially hope that we're not the run they're gearing up to bomb."

Jack and Maggie didn't stay long in the park. The sound was too annoying. They walked back to the house, but they could hear the sound there, too. Maggie went into Desert Bloomers, turned on music, and closed the door. She did paperwork and made stock bottles from mother flower essence bottles.

Before she realized it, it was dinner time.

She left Desert Bloomers and knocked on Jack's door. No one answered. She went around to the front of the bunkhouse. Jack was sitting with his feet up on the railing, his eyes half-shut.

"Hey, Jack," Maggie said. "Time for dinner. You seen Anders?"

Jack dropped his feet and stood and stretched. "No, I haven't seen him all day."

"Hmmm, I hope he didn't wander away," Maggie said.

"He said he could take care of himself," Jack said. "Told me he knows how to be invisible."

Maggie laughed. "Now that would be a skill." She looked around. "Anders! Where are you?" She listened for an answer. "He loves eating so much. I'd hate for him to miss dinner. Though come to think of it, I missed lunch, so he probably did, too. Could he be in the bunkhouse?"

Jack opened the door and looked inside. "Not there."

"Anders!" Maggie walked away from the barn. "Jack, will you check the garden? I know he's working hard to get my garden into shape. I'll check the house just in case."

"Sure thing, partner," Jack said.

Maggie went into the house. It was the first time she'd been inside for hours. On the kitchen table were several plates with bits of food on them. And the kitchen itself was wrecked: plates, pots, food scattered everywhere.

"What the—?"

Had looters hit her house while she was in Desert Bloomers?

She heard a sound coming from her bedroom. Her stomach lurched. Were they still here?

She picked up one of the pots by its long handle. She slowly walked toward the bedroom.

She peeked into the darkened room. Someone was on her bed. Naked.

"Hello?" Maggie said.

The figure turned around and sat up. "Hello!"

Anders.

"Jesus H. Christ," Maggie said as she put down the pot. "What are you doing? And why is my house trashed?"

Anders frowned. "Trashed?" He stood.

"Put on some clothes," Maggie said as she averted her gaze.

"It's so uncomfortable," he said. He had a slight accent again. "The clothes. I feel as though I cannot breathe."

"Maybe we can find you better fitting clothes at John's or Ricardo's," Maggie said. "But for right now, put on some clothes. Or try some of mine. Look in my dresser there. Come out when you're dressed."

Maggie pulled the door closed behind her. Then she began cleaning up the kitchen and dining area. Someone knocked on the front door, and she heard Jack calling to her. She shouted for him to come in.

"Wow," he said as he walked into the living room. "You must have been hungry this morning."

"This isn't from me," Maggie said. "It's from our visitor. I guess he got hungry and then he got sleepy. Or vice versa. And he got naked."

Jack nodded. "I figured he had eyes for you. I've seen the way you two are together."

"I don't know what you're talking about," Maggie said. She began rinsing off dishes and stacking them in the sink.

"Animal magnetism," Jack said. "You go to him like he's steel and you're a magnet. Or something like. I understand. He is a beautiful man—or whatever he is. If I was inclined that way, I might have a looksee myself."

"Anything you'd like to see is on display in my room right now," Maggie said.

The door to the bedroom opened. Maggie kept her back to it.

"Here I am," Anders said.

"It's safe, Mags," Jack said.

Maggie turned around.

Anders was dressed in a pair of her gray sweatpants and a purple blouse.

"That's awfully purty, Anders," Jack said.

"It smells like Maggie," he said. "I like it."

Maggie had never seen a man in a purple blouse before.

"Anders, that's a woman's shirt," she said.

"What?"

"That's my blouse," Maggie said. "It's for a woman, not a man."

"But it's a beautiful color," Anders said.

"I know, but it's not something a man would wear."

"I am wearing it."

Maggie made a noise.

"What does it matter?" Jack asked. "He's comfortable in it. Might as well wear it."

"Wouldn't a T-shirt be just as comfortable?"

"Mags, I think we're discovering that you have some

definite ideas about what's male and what's female," Jack said.

"A T-shirt?" Anders said. He pointed to Jack. "Is that a T-shirt."

"Yes, sir," Jack said. "What planet you come from anyway that you don't know what a T-shirt is?" He stopped. "I forgot who I was speaking to. Yes, this is a T-shirt. I've got a few more. You want to try one? Make Maggie more comfortable."

"I don't care what he wears," Maggie said. "I was just telling him it was woman's shirt. Don't know why it's a woman's shirt."

Jack and Anders walked toward the front door.

"I was just educating him," Maggie said.

"Whatever you say, darlin'," Jack said.

Maggie threw the dish towel at the sink as the front door closed behind them. Wouldn't Joanna get a kick out of this?

If Maggie ever told her.

Eight of them met at John and Nina's house—Alicia was eating at her friend Carolla's house. Nearly every inch of John and Nina's living room walls were covered with NASA photographs and grainy pictures of flying saucers. Jack walked around the living room with his mouth open.

"I know, I know," Nina said. "We need to move these photos into another room so that new people don't think we're completely looney tunes. Old friends already know we're looney tunes." She laughed.

Maggie went into the kitchen.

"Need any help?" Maggie asked.

"Just carry stuff into the dining room," John said.

She helped take chicken hotdogs, soy hotdogs, potato salad, and a Thai salad with rice noodles into the dinning room. Lisa grabbed the buns and catsup and whispered to Maggie as she went by, "We're going to have to have a discussion on what kind of food we're going to eat. Hot dogs? Oh my god."

Soon they were all seated around the table, with Nina at one end and John at the other. Maggie ran her fingertips over the tablecloth. It had been a long time since she'd seen a tablecloth. Maybe since she had lived in the Midwest. This one was cotton with pale pink flowers. Most people had beautiful wooden tables here and didn't cover them up with cloth, except maybe a colorful runner down the middle now and again

"I'm so glad you're all here," Nina said. "We've never had this many people over! Maybe disasters do make good friends." She laughed. "I don't mean disasters make good friends. I mean in times of disaster we can find good friends. Anyway, let's eat." She looked across the table at Anders and said loudly, "Anders, these are hotdogs. They are not really made from dogs. Those ones there are made from chickens, however, and those here from soybeans. Soybeans never had a mother, but the chickens did."

"Technically everything has a mother," Lisa said. "I don't think everything has a father, but a mother, yes. Has to happen. We give birth. Without us, there is no creation. Another reason those creation myths without a female are so ridiculous. Pass me the potato salad, please. Is there anything green to eat, Nina?"

Maggie glanced over at Joanna. She looked tired and a bit ragged. Her clothes were disheveled and strands of hair fell down from her braid and into her face.

"Any news from Alex?" Maggie asked her.

Joanna shook her head. "I couldn't get a hold of her all day. This is all so frustrating."

"Tell me about it," John said. "If Nina and I aren't able to work soon I'm afraid we'll be fired."

Nina nodded. "Our bosses don't care that there's a rift. They want us to go over the rift!" She laughed and shook her head. "If only we could."

"Maybe we can," Maggie said. "I don't know if you heard, but they took the nonresidents over the rift last night."

John, Nina, and Joanna looked at one another and then at Maggie.

"You should have told us," Joanna said.

"I thought I'd see you at Desert Bloomers today," Maggie said. "And I'm sorry, John and Nina, it didn't occur to me."

"We're supposed to be sharing information," John said.

"Yes, I know, you're right," Maggie said. "I'm sorry. My brain doesn't seem to be firing on all cylinders these days."

"Bill Boyle tried to get them to take Tilly," Lisa said. "They wouldn't. He was pissed off."

"You're gonna get sick you keep eating that way," Jack said to Anders. "Chew your food a bit. It'll be better for you that way. Plus the ladies will like you if you have some table manners."

Anders wiped catsup and mustard off his mouth with his napkin.

"I am so sorry," he said. He still seemed to have a slight accent. French maybe. "But your food is so good."

Nina grinned. "That is so nice of you!"

"Man, if he fucks like he eats," Lisa said, "he'd be some kind of wonderful."

"Oh my word," Joanna said.

Ricardo laughed.

"What? Come on?" Lisa said. "A woman likes enthusiasm. And he is an enthusiastic eater yet he still has that delicious looking body. Don't you think, Maggie?"

"Hey, leave me out of this," Maggie said. "You're talking about him as though he isn't here. He's sitting right across the table from you."

"Have I offended you, Anders?" Lisa asked.

Anders waited until he swallowed and then he said, "I don't think so. I was chewing this amazing hot dog thing and couldn't concentrate on anything else. I don't know how you can eat and talk and think at the same time!"

"He is exactly right," Nina said. "We should be in the now and do one thing at a time."

"Oh good lord," Lisa said.

"I went down to the rift today," Ricardo said. "They are going to start food drops tomorrow morning. I asked if we need to give them a list of what we want and Shaw said no."

"Which means they're going to bring us crap," Lisa said. "And this brings me to tonight's dinner."

"Which is very good," Maggie said.

"Finest potato salad I have ever had," Jack said. "I especially liked the hint of vinegar in there."

"Old family recipe," John said.

"Yes, all that," Lisa said. "But I'm wondering if we should make a menu that we all stick to. I tried to get you all to help me with the menu last night, but you ran away too soon. This meal isn't going to keep us going until tomorrow. I'd like more substantial meals, rather than picnic dinners."

Everyone was silent for a moment.

"Or better yet," Lisa said. "We could put all the supplies at our house and meet there every day for dinner. We could still take turns cooking and cleaning, but I would volunteer to be coordinator."

"Seems like a lot of trouble to haul all of our food stuff over to your place," John said, "especially given we have no transportation."

"I think they're going to turn off the electricity next," Lisa said. "We're the only ones with a generator. Everything will spoil if you keep it at your houses."

"But then only you will have the food," Nina said.

"What does that mean?" Lisa asked.

"It means you'll have the food," Nina said. "And if you get pissed at us for any reason, you might not let us have it."

"Are you fucking kidding me?" Lisa asked.

"Hey," Maggie said. "It's a fair question."

Lisa put her right hand in the air, as though she was taking an oath.

"I promise that no matter how pissed off I get at any of you assholes, I'll let you have your own food back. There, are you satisfied?"

"I still think it sounds like a lot of work," Joanna said. "We'll be out of here soon. And then we'll have to get it all back again. I live a bit a ways from here, remember."

"What about your neighborhood anyway?" Lisa asked. "What are they doing there? Is everyone helping everyone out?"

"People have been making sure everyone has enough hay for their horses," Joanna said. "Not much has been said about the people."

"You should be careful up there in that big house all alone," Lisa said. "There could be looters."

"Why would you say that?" Joanna asked. "You've got to know I'm not happy being there alone."

"You got a gun, right?" Lisa asked.

"Leave her alone," Ricardo said. "Why do you have to be such a hard ass now? Leave everyone alone. We are all doing the best we can."

"I don't think people understand what's happening," Lisa said. "Did you hear the jets today? That roar. That noise? What do you think they're getting fired up about? Us. They're fired up about us. They think we're all a bunch of terrorists."

"Is that what that noise was?" Nina asked.

"It comes from the Air Force base, but we don't really know what it is," Maggie said.

"Why would they think any of us are terrorists?" John asked. "We didn't cause the rift."

"We don't know what caused the rift," Lisa said. "They don't either. For all we know, it could have been caused by idiot savant Anders here. Maybe they're looking for him."

Jack looked over at Maggie. She put down her fork.

"They are not looking for Anders," Maggie said.

"Maybe we should tell them about Anders," Nina said. "They would protect him. If people on this side think he's a terrorist they might hurt him. At least the government would protect him. He could be the only one in the whole universe like him."

"There'd have to be more," John said, "because someone sent him. Think it through, baby."

"I'm just saying it might be for his own good."

"They'll experiment on him," John said. "Take pieces of him to test."

Even Anders had stopped eating.

Nina started to cry. "I don't know what to do," she said. "It seems like everything is falling apart. I just want it back to normal."

"We all do," Joanna said. "Don't let Lisa, or anyone else, frighten you. It will be over soon."

"Is that more of your New Age bullshit optimism?" Lisa asked.

"Are you turning into Wendell Davies?" Joanna asked. "As Maggie pointed out, what we do is definitely 'old age,' not New Age."

"And here's another thing," Lisa said. "I don't want y'all calling on Ricardo every time you want to be driven somewhere. He is not your goddamn chauffeur. We need to save the gasoline for emergencies."

"What emergencies?" Maggie said. "We're already in an emergency and it's not like you could drive anyone to a hospital."

"Maybe this sharing of community resources wasn't such a great idea since we seem to be the only ones sharing," Lisa said.

"Lisa," Joanna said. "What is wrong with you? Nina and John made this meal for us."

"Why are you fighting?" Anders asked. "We're all together eating this beautiful meal. Shouldn't we be happy?"

"The dude's gotta point," Jack said. "Smile and be happy. And eat some grub, man."

NEXT

After dinner, four of them played Scrabble and four of them played cards. Anders loved Scrabble. He thought of what word he was going to put down for a long while. Fortunately, Lisa was playing cards. Jack, Nina, and Maggie didn't care how long Anders took.

By the time the party broke up, they all seemed to be friends again. Or as friendly as they ever were.

As Maggie walked back toward home in the dark with Anders and Jack, she realized that she had been friends with Lisa and Ricardo all these years because she liked Ricardo—so she tolerated Lisa. And Joanna. She loved Joanna, but she had never noticed how willing she was to go along to get along.

Maggie didn't like either strategy: being obnoxious just to be obnoxious or going along just to keep the peace. Although, actually, Joanna had stood up for Nina and John. Maggie hadn't said much. She'd been surprised by the whole thing: She was surprised at how quickly good intentions came undone.

When they got to Javalina Road, Maggie said, "I'll meet you guys at home. I want to go down to the rift."

"I'd like to see the rift," Anders said. "You have been talking about it so much."

Jack put his hand on Anders's shoulder. "Maybe another time, dude, when the *federalos* aren't around." He nodded to Maggie. Anders shrugged and the two men walked away.

Maggie walked down toward the rift. The flashing lights splashed the desert in Christmas colors. Off and on, off and on. As she got closer, she saw two armed figures on either side of the road on the west side of the rift.

Someone got out of the squad car and walked toward her: Shaw. The armed guards were dressed in riot gear, their faces covered by a plastic shield, their heads protected by a helmet, their bulky suits black. Not really desert gear.

Maggie saw one of the guards twitch, as though he wanted to shoot. Her. She thought she heard Shaw say something to them.

And then Maggie and Shaw were looking at each other from across the rift.

"You came and took all the nonresidents away," Maggie said. "Where'd they go?"

"Home," he said. "Now, like you and your friends, they are safe in the confines of their homes."

"I guess you *can* travel over the rift," she said.

"Yes, we can," he said. "The aircraft was equipped with a few necessary safety devices."

"So you can take people from here over to there," Maggie said.

"If there is an emergency we can take people," Shaw said, "but for now, until we get this cleared up, we feel it's better for everyone's safety if the residents of the east side stay on the east side."

"People have jobs," Maggie said.

"We understand that," Shaw said. "We're working as quickly as possible."

"Really?" Maggie said. Who was this guy? Why was he always there? Didn't he sleep?

Shaw nodded. "Things would go more quickly if we had the terrorist," he said. "Then we would be better equipped to determine if the east side is now safe."

"It must be safe," she said. "We're living here. And I haven't seen any terrorists. What do you think this so-called terrorist did?"

He looked down at the rift.

"A terrorist caused this?" Maggie asked.

"Among other things which are top secret."

Maggie gazed beyond Shaw. She tried to imagine the stores that lined Speedway all the way to the freeway, for miles and miles and miles. She did not miss any of it. Strange.

"We'll drop off food tomorrow," he said. "You'll see. It'll be good."

"What's with the armed guards?"

"Security," he said. "We want to make certain you're all protected."

"If they're protecting us," Maggie said, "shouldn't they be turned the other way?"

"Danger often comes from within," Shaw said.

"I bet you're nostalgic for the fifties," Maggie said.

"I don't know what you mean," he said.

"See you tomorrow," Maggie said.

Maggie hurried home. Something about her exchange with Shaw seemed ominous. The light was on under the bunkhouse door and off under the Desert Bloomers door. She thought about asking Jack in for tea, but she didn't want to make it into a habitual thing. A routine. She didn't want him to start expecting anything from her.

She went into the house and found every container she could find and then filled them with water. When she was finished, she kicked off her shoes and padded into the bedroom.

Anders was lying in her bed, on top of the covers. This time, Maggie wasn't surprised.

"I kept my clothes on," he said. "Just for you."

"Don't do me any favors," she said.

He cocked his head as though he didn't quite understand. She wasn't going to explain it to him: He was nice to look at, with or without clothes.

"What are you doing here?" Maggie asked.

"I want to be here tonight," he said. "Usually I walk in the desert, but tonight I want to be here with you."

"Oh, so you've been wandering the desert at night," she said. "How do you see?"

"How do you not see?" he said. The answer sounded metaphoric; she had meant it practically.

"You may not need to sleep," Maggie said, "but I do. I'm exhausted."

"I will stay here with you," Anders said. "Maybe I will sleep, too."

For some reason Maggie couldn't explain, she said, "All right. But don't hog the covers. I've missed sleeping with someone since Irving died. I wouldn't mind the company."

"Splendid!" Anders said. Now he seemed to have an English accent.

Maggie began unbuttoning her shirt.

"Does that mean I can get naked now, too?" Anders said.

Maggie laughed. "I'm putting on pajamas." She usually slept in her panties and camisole, but she decided she'd wear a little extra. "Do you want a pair?"

Anders grimaced. "Why are your clothes so clingy?"

"My clothes aren't tight," Maggie said. She took off her shirt, dropped it in the dirty clothes basket, and then opened the dresser and pulled out a pair of red cotton pjs. She took off her jeans and then slipped on the pajama bottoms.

"You are beautiful," Anders said. "Why cover it up?"

Maggie shrugged. She pulled down the covers and got into bed.

Anders pulled off his T-shirt and then got under the covers with Maggie. They faced one another.

"Tell me everything," Anders said.

Maggie stared into his green, green eyes.

"What's to tell?"

"It's true," Anders said. "Words are often inadequate."

He held his hand out to her. She put her hand in his. They folded their fingers together.

They breathed together.

And breathed.

He had the most amazing green eyes. She could fall

into them, like falling in a stormy sea—no, like falling into a calm sea. Or a jewel. It was like when she closed her eyes and felt as though the plants all around her were reaching out to her. Plants. *Nothing would exist without plants, without them breathing out and digesting in and breathing out; every animal got nourishment from plants, even if it was secondhand: the man ate the cow who ate the plants who . . . or maybe looking into Anders's eyes was like when she sensed the plant spirits around her, or the desert spirits, knowing, always knowing that she needn't be lonely because plants were everywhere, like the devas, the faeries, the beings from other realms, only why was she thinking any of this, thought was not important, feeling was important and she didn't feel much these days, wasn't sure why, because her dog died, because she realized she missed human companionship, because something was missing, wasn't sure what, even now she felt like she could fall into Anders's arms, as though he was a cloud, a ball of light, a being from another planet, she needed solidity, didn't need anything, didn't need to fix anything, didn't care about the past, wasn't confused about the present, wasn't worried about the future, shhhh, the world was purring and holy green light infused her . . .*

Anders saw everything.

Maggie wasn't sure she saw anything, but it did not matter.

Not now.

When Maggie awakened, she was curled up against Anders. His arms were wrapped around her. She tensed for a moment and then relaxed and snuggled deeper into him.

She closed her eyes. She didn't want this feeling to go away, but she could already feel herself shifting. She could feel herself judging. How strange this was. How peculiar to spend the night with a complete stranger looking into his eyes and then falling to sleep in his arms. What good was this? What end to it?

She turned around so she was facing Anders. He opened his eyes and smiled at her.

"Thank you for letting me dream with you," Anders said.

"We dreamed together?" Maggie said. "I don't remember."

"Yes," he said. "We were naked together. We made love all night long."

"In the dreams or in real life?" Maggie asked.

"Does it make a difference?" he asked.

"Uh, yes, it actually does."

"In the dreams," Anders said. "But we could bring the dreams into real life."

Maggie smiled. "Maybe—"

Someone was banging on her front door again.

"Mags!"

Jack's voice.

"Shit," she said. She got out of bed, pulled slacks over her pajamas and put on a shirt. Then she hurried to the door. She opened it and stepped outside.

The sun was bright already. She must have slept in again.

Ricardo stood next to Jack.

"What's wrong?" she asked.

"The electricity is off," Ricardo said. "Has been since early this morning. We've called, but the line is still busy. We've got our generator, but no one else does.

We need to get the frozen goods into our refrigerator. And another helicopter came. Dropped food at Speedway and Broadway. Lisa's there now."

Jack squinted as he looked at Maggie, as though he knew something about her.

"Okay," she said. "Let me get dressed."

"But you are dressed," Jack said.

"Uh, then I'll be right out."

She went inside. Jack tried to look inside as she shut the door. She ran back to the bedroom. Anders was curled up under the covers.

"I've got to go," she said, "but you stay here. I think you need to stay out of sight."

He peeked his head out. "I know how to be invisible."

She nodded. "That's a skill you'll have to teach me one day."

She changed her clothes, then ran outside, and got into the front of the truck with Jack and Ricardo.

"What's going on with you this morning, Mags?" Jack said. "You seem a little mysterious."

"Aren't I always mysterious?" Maggie asked.

"I haven't seen Anders around," he said. "You?"

"I told him to stay out of sight," Maggie said. "It feels like something's changed today."

Jack nodded. "I wouldn't argue with you about that."

Dozens of people had gathered a short distance from the rift, going through the piles of containers the helicopter had apparently dropped.

Maggie got out of the truck when it stopped. Lisa came over to them.

"It's powdered milk, cheddar cheese in a box, white bread," Lisa said. "Some canned stuff. All crap."

Maggie watched as her neighbors picked through the boxes.

"Maybe we should take some just in case," Maggie said.

"You bet your ass," Lisa said. "We can use them to barter later on."

"Later on?" Maggie said. "How long do you think we're going to be here?"

"It's been four days," Lisa said. "Or five. I've lost track."

"Is that all?" Maggie said. "It feels like weeks."

Maggie went over to the supplies and got the bread, some canned goods, and cheese: Anders would eat anything. As she started back to the truck, she glanced over at the rift. Shaw was watching her. She handed her supplies to Jack and then walked to the rift.

"What's going on with the electricity?" Maggie asked.

"A transformer blew," Shaw said. "They're working on it."

"I've heard that before," Maggie said.

"Why are you so hostile?" Shaw asked.

"Do I seem hostile?" Maggie asked. "Maybe it's because we're cut off from society, we don't have any fresh food, and now the electricity is gone, so we can't get water or use the toilets."

"I thought you didn't especially like society," he said.

"You don't know anything about me," Maggie said. "I think you have the power to fix this road and our electricity. Tell us what needs to happen for us to get our electricity back."

"We're very concerned about a terrorist cell in the area," he said. "We still don't have an accurate count of all the people in the east end."

"That's because your phones are always busy," she said.

"If you could get a group of people to go house to house and get an accurate count, I think I could get them to begin the roadwork."

"And turn the electricity back on," Maggie said.

"As I indicated, they are working on that," he said. "Remember, it's your government. We're working for you."

"The state of Arizona is working for me?" Maggie asked. "It's not working fast enough."

"The federal government is now the lead agency on this," Shaw said.

That was a good thing. The federal government wouldn't be so caught up in bureaucratic good ol' boy-isms, right? They could come in and get things done.

Or it meant things had deteriorated so badly that only the feds could help. Maybe there really had been some kind of toxic accident or terrorist attack.

"I can't go door to door on the entire east side," Maggie said. "For one thing, I can't get there because the roads don't go all the way through."

"If you could get the information from your area, between Speedway and Broadway, that would be helpful."

"All right, I will go door to door and get what you need," Maggie said. Not that she had any intention of telling him anything about Anders. "As long as work begins on the rift and the electricity comes back on."

Shaw nodded.

Maggie went back to the truck. Joanna had shown up on Boxer. Boxer's saddlebags looked like they were loaded with food.

"Are you going to eat any of that?" Maggie asked.

"If I get hungry enough," Joanna said. "I've got to keep my strength up and we didn't have much food in the house."

"You can come eat anything in my house," Maggie said. "Look, everyone, I talked to Shaw. He said that if we get an accurate count of everyone on the east side, they'll start repairs to the road and restore electricity."

"He told you this?" Lisa asked. "Why'd he tell you? You two seem kind of palsy-walsy."

"I don't know why he tells me things," Maggie said. "Maybe because I ask him. I think we should break up into groups, two to a group at least to be safe, and then let's just ask people if they're willing to say how many people they've got in their homes. I don't know why they need this info, but I don't think it can hurt to ask."

"You gonna tell them about your space alien?" Lisa asked.

"I'll tell them how many people we've got at my place," Maggie said.

"It'd be faster on horseback," Joanna said. "You can come up and get Crazy Lu if you like."

Maggie nodded. "Ricardo and Jack, you could go together. Shouldn't take us too long."

Ricardo nodded. "All right, let's split up the district."

Ricardo got a map from his glove compartment. "We'll go up here," he pointed, "and you and Joanna down here."

Maggie nodded. "We'll meet at dinner, compile the info, and then I'll take it down to Shaw. Where is dinner tonight?"

"Are we still doing that?" Lisa said. "Everyone seemed so hostile last night."

No one said anything for a moment. Then Maggie said, "Lisa, if you could tone down your hostility toward everyone, we could keep having dinner together."

"Did a little plant spirit tell you that?"

Maggie shook her head.

"To answer your question, we were supposed to have dinner at Joanna's tonight," Lisa said. "But that's a long way to schlep food."

"I don't care if we have it someplace else," Joanna said. "I'm not much in the mood for cooking anyway."

"My place it is then," Lisa said. "For one thing, we're the only ones with electricity. Jack, you gonna help again?"

Jack glanced at Maggie. Then he said.

"At your service, always."

Maggie got on Boxer, behind Joanna, and they rode to her house, saying little to one another. Once there, they went inside the house so Joanna could get her sun hat. The air was still and stale, as though a window hadn't been cracked in a long time. And the house smelled a bit like cat piss. Unwashed dishes were strewn across the countertop.

"You need me to help with anything around here?" Maggie called to Joanna. "This is a big house to keep up on your own."

Joanna came into the room carrying two sun hats. She handed one to Maggie.

"Are you trying to tell me something?" Joanna asked. She glanced around. "I guess it is a little messy."

"Just smells a little stale," Maggie said.

"I've been a bit nervous here on my own," Joanna said. "But I didn't want to say that to anyone. I miss Alexandria. She's the tough one, you know. Never afraid of anything."

"I've never noticed you're afraid of much," Maggie said.

"Yeah, that's cuz I'm in my own little world," Joanna said. "And in your world. Us with the plants. Feels really fragile now with this going on."

They went outside again. Joanna saddled Crazy Lu. Maggie stood at the horse's head and talked to her as Joanna tightened the cinch strap. When she was finished, both women got on their horses and started down the road.

"If you really think about it," Maggie said, "not much has changed."

Joanna laughed. "You're kidding, right? My partner is gone, there's a hole in the earth, we've got no electricity, water, or food. We may or may not have been exposed to some kind of toxic substance and we may or may not be under terrorist attack. I'd say some things have changed."

"Right this second, we have enough water and food," Maggie said. "And we've got each other."

"If we don't kill each other first," Joanna said.

At first, Maggie and Joanna both got off their horses and walked to the door of each house together. Then they explained to the residents that they could get the electricity back and the road fixed if they could get an accurate count of how many people were still in the east end. After a while, they started taking turns. One would stay on her horse and one would get off her horse. Most people happily gave them the names of each person in the house and how many people were there. Two or three people came to the door with shotgun in hand. Joan Doud was one of them. But she did say she and Gabriel were the only ones at home.

"We should also get a count of the strange creatures running about since the rift," Joan said. "There are crows everywhere."

"There are always crows everywhere," Maggie said.

"Now there are more," she said. "And ravens. And some strange black horse. And a naked man running through the wash."

"I don't know anything about any of that," Maggie said. "Just want to get this info to the feds and maybe get our roads fixed."

Joan Doud closed the door. Maggie got back up on Crazy Lu.

"I used to think the world was a kind and beautiful place," Joanna said. "But now seeing our neighbors come to the door with guns. And to see how quickly our friends become assholes. It's really very disheartening. I feel as though I've lived in this bubble all this time and I'm just beginning to see the real world."

"Our neighbors have always had guns," Maggie said. "And our friends have always been assholes."

Joanna laughed. "That's reassuring. I really miss Alexandria. I think of all the times I've been pissed at her, or annoyed with her, and now all I want is to see her again and apologize for any stupid thing I've done over the years."

"You'll see her soon enough," Maggie said as they turned the horses toward the next house down the road. This was horse country so the houses were spread far apart from one another with plenty of desert in-between. "Joan's right about the crows though." She nodded toward a grove of mesquite trees. "There they are again. They line up there near dusk. Seem to be watching the sunset, or the rift. And I've seen that black horse. I actually think it's more blue than black."

"Horse of a different color."

Maggie nodded.

They didn't stop at Bill and Tilly's house. Maggie knew how many people lived there. They met Ricardo at his house and he gave her his totals and the names. Maggie rode Crazy Lu back to the rift as the sun was setting. She got off the horse and went to stand at the edge of the rift. In the distance, she saw huge yellow trucks heading east: road repair equipment.

Shaw got out of the car and came to stand across from her.

"You need the names or the total?" she asked. "If you could get the internet working I could email you the names."

"Just the total for now," he said.

She gave him the total, minus one.

"Does that jive with what you expected?" she asked.

He looked up at her. "Keep the list of everyone's names," he said. "We might need it later."

"How long will it take to repair the road?" Maggie asked.

"Shouldn't take long."

Maggie got back on the horse and headed to Ricardo's house.

She didn't believe a word Shaw said.

Maggie heard laughter coming from the kitchen when she walked into Lisa and Ricardo's house. She went by the TV which was tuned to the public access channel. On the screen were the words "Please Stay Tuned."

Ricardo, Lisa, Joanna, and Jack were standing around the kitchen.

"You notice anything?" Joanna asked.

Maggie looked around.

"The lights, the lights!" Lisa said. "They came on a half 'n hour ago. We've already started dinner—just in case it goes out again. We'll have a feast. You want to help with dinner?"

Maggie shook her head. "Not tonight, dear. I've got a headache."

Lisa laughed.

Anders stepped out of the pantry and into the kitchen. He had blueberry stains on his lips.

"I have never tasted anything like this," Anders said. "Can I eat more?"

"You're like a three year old," Lisa said. "Come here and let me wipe that off of you."

Jack touched Maggie's arm and said quietly, "I need to talk to you."

She nodded, and she and Jack left the kitchen and walked through the living room just as Nina and John were coming inside.

"Hello!" Nina said. "Isn't this great? The electricity is back on! Things are looking up."

"Yep," Maggie said.

Jack and Maggie stepped outside and walked over to stand near the paloverde by the corrals.

"What's up?" Maggie asked.

"Anders and I were walking around the neighborhood," he said. "I know you don't want anyone to see him, but he was determined, so I went with. Didn't see another living soul. But we went by one of those light poles down Speedway a bit. He was asking me about electricity and why we need it and stuff. Then he walked up to this pole and put this hands on it. I think that's when the electricity came back on."

"The electricity was probably back on and you just didn't know it," Maggie said.

Jack shrugged. "I dunno. He is a very strange dude."

"Yeah, well, *you* may or may not be a coyote," Maggie said.

He laughed. "And *you* are pretty darn protective of him."

"I feel like he needs it," she said.

Jack shook his head. "I'm not sure. I think you may need protecting from him."

"Anders wouldn't hurt a flea," Maggie said.

"Your eyes just light up when you see him," Jack said. "I know what it's like to get your heart broke."

Maggie laughed. "It's not that way. I don't feel that way about him. I just feel very comfortable around him, in a strange uncomfortable way."

"Whatever you say," Jack said. "I just thought you should know."

"So does this mean you think he's from outer space?" Maggie asked.

Jack shrugged. "I have no idea. As far as I know, the

government could have sent him here to spy on us, to see how we deal with change, or with intruders. It could be an experiment. Everything started when he showed up."

"No it didn't, Jack," Maggie said. "It all started when you showed up."

"I like the little fellah," Jack said. "I feel protective around him, too. But my loyalty is with you. After all, you saved my life."

"You weren't dying," Maggie said. "You just needed some care."

"And you gave it to me," Jack said. "Not everyone is willing to put their hands on another human being. Not everyone is willing to take another soul into their soul. And that's what you did."

"You make me sound much nicer than I am," she said. "I was just doing my job."

"Now you're dismissing me because I've made you uncomfortable," he said.

"I thought it was the woman who was supposed to analyze everything to death, Jack."

"Like I said before, you've got some notions about men and women."

"I don't want to hear about that purple blouse again," she said.

Jack put her arm across Maggie's shoulders and squeezed her as they started back to the house.

"He had a pink shirt on today," Jack said, "but I gave him one of my T-shirts again. He's just picking from your closest, Mags, and I gotta tell ya, you've got some girlie clothes in there."

The meal seemed more relaxed than it had the night before, yet Maggie felt something underneath it all. A tension. Fear. Weariness. Except for Anders. He happily ate Lisa's enchiladas, tamales, tacos, and commented on the smells, the taste, the sounds. Maggie started paying more attention to her food. She smelled it first. Chewed it well. She worked with plants all day, yet she rarely paid any attention to her food, except for the blessing before she began cooking and before she began eating. She had started doing so many things by rote. How had that happened?

Why?

Sometimes she felt like there was so much to heal in the world, and she did not have the resources to do it any more.

Not that she ever had.

When had she started taking on the burden of saving the world?

All of her life.

Maggie put down her fork. Jack and Anders were laughing. Anders had red sauce all over his lips. Lisa rolled her eyes.

When Maggie was a girl, she thought she needed to fix everything. Make it better for everyone in her family. Make everyone happy. That sense of responsibility had driven her further and further away from home.

Until she barely saw her family any more. In fact, she hadn't even called them since the rift happened. And they had not called her. Not her father or either of her two sisters. They must know what was happening. It had to be on all the 24-hour news channels. Didn't it?

She picked up her fork again and ate a mouthful of enchiladas. She could taste the corn, potatoes, carrots, cilantro. *They had used cilantro.* She probably wouldn't have noticed that a day ago.

She always told her clients to slow down, to be in the now, to smell the desert roses—to become desert bloomers. And here she was forgetting to notice her food. Forgetting to honor that which gave her nourishment.

Anders leaned over and kissed Maggie on the cheek with his red-stained lips.

"Oh!" Maggie said.

Everyone laughed. Maggie wiped her cheek off with her napkin. She glanced at John who was sitting on her right.

"What are you laughing about?"

She put her fingers in the red sauce on her plate and smeared it on her lips. Then she kissed John's cheek.

"Ick!" he said as he wiped it off.

Then he passed it onto Nina until the messy kiss went all around the table—almost stopping when it came to Lisa. The hoots and hollering pressured her into continuing the kiss. When it came back to Anders, everyone cheered.

He was the only one who didn't wipe off the kiss.

NEXT

Maggie invited Joanna to spend the night, so they rode Crazy Lu and Boxer back to the house while Anders and Jack walked beside them. Twilight made everything fuzzy, not quite covered in darkness, not quite light enough to make anything distinct.

They crossed the wash, and then the women got off the horses. Maggie started to throw Crazy Lu's reins over the corral fence when she heard a familiar dog bark.

She looked over her shoulders and saw a black dog running through the wash.

"Irving?"

She ran after the dog. Didn't hesitate. One part of her brain was screaming, "He's dead! He's dead!" The other part was telling her to run, run.

"Irving!" she called as she ran. The black shape seemed to hesitate, jump, and then keep going. Maggie realized too late why the animal had hesitated. She tried to pull herself up. Tried to stop, but momentum was the quantity of motion measured by . . .

Maggie ran right into the barbed wire fence, groaned and bounced back and onto the ground.

She tried to turn her face to look down the wash—to see the dog. But the gray had bled out, and night settled into the wash in that instant.

In the next moment, Jack, Anders, and Joanna were by Maggie's side. They said words, but Maggie wasn't clear what they were. It was all happening so quickly. They lifted her and carried her back to the house. Maggie was groggy, and their hands felt warm and tingly, like little sparks of electricity running from their fingers and into her body.

She hurt like hell.

They carried her into Desert Bloomers. The light stung her eyes.

"Shit," Jack said.

"Good poker face," Maggie said.

She looked down. Across her chest and upper forearms were pinpricks of blood. She could feel where the fence had gotten her across her abdomen, but she didn't see anything.

"Anders, you stay with your hands on her head," Joanna said, "and Jack, stay at her feet. Maggie, let's take off your clothes."

Joanna went to the shelf and came back with arnica in homeopathic pellets and a bottle of rescue remedy. She dropped the pellets under Maggie's tongue and then squeezed drops of the rescue remedy into her mouth. Joanna helped Maggie out of her shirt and her jeans. Maggie didn't care if Jack and Anders saw her in her camisole and underwear. She'd already spent the night with Anders, and Jack had already seen her naked in his imagination, so what was the difference?

Joanna gently washed the places where the barbed wire had broken the skin. Then she brushed the wounds with alcohol.

"Not so bad," Joanna said. "Some bruising, a little blood. The arnica should help. What were you doing?" She reached under the table for a blanket and then spread it over Maggie. Maggie closed her eyes. Anders's hands on her head still felt tingly. Jack's hands were warm. Joanna put her hands over Maggie's abdominal area, a few inches above her body.

"I thought I saw Irving," Maggie said, "and I just forgot about the fence."

"Irving is the dog," Anders said.

Maggie opened her eyes and looked up at Anders. His eyes were so green. Like lights. That couldn't be natural, could it? Couldn't be from this world. She didn't care, though. She liked looking into his eyes. Felt like she was falling into that comforting sea again.

"Irving was my dog," Maggie said. "He's dead."

"So you know it couldn't have been him," Joanna said. "We buried him."

"I know," Maggie said. She closed her eyes. "It was stupid. It just sounded like him and looked like him. And a lot of weird things have happened. For one, there's the rift. For another, a coyote has turned into a man and I rescued a naked man—or alien or faery or something—from the wash. And no one in the rest of the world seems to want to do anything about what's going on here."

"Not true," Joanna said. "Alexandria is trying to get someone to do something."

Maggie felt cool heat traveling down her body—like

when her mother rubbed Vicks on her chest when she was a girl.

Jack squeezed her feet. She smiled. Felt like she had known Jack all of her life. He wanted her to know that he was still there. Still waiting for a love potion, no doubt.

Suddenly Maggie felt like she couldn't stay on the table any longer.

She had to get up.

To get out.

"Okay, I'm done," Maggie said. "Hand me my clothes. Thank you all."

The three moved away from her, and Maggie sat up. Joanna gave her her clothes. Maggie pulled on her jeans, then hopped down from the table and put on her shirt. She pushed her feet into her shoes.

"Good night," Maggie said.

She left Desert Bloomers.

Then she remembered the horses and Joanna. She looked back at the three of them watching her.

"I forgot about the horses," she said. "Can you take care of them? I'm going to take a bath. Soak in some Epsom salts. Joanna, you know where your room is. See you in the morning."

She didn't understand what was going on, but she had to get away.

Too much happening in the last few days. Too many people around.

Maggie took a bath, then a shower to wash off the Epsom salts. Afterward, she closed the shades in her room and crawled into bed. She was glad Anders wasn't there. It had been fun having a bed buddy for one night. Like the sleepovers she had had when she was a girl. Now she wanted to be alone.

Maggie dreamed someone shot her at point blank range. She sat up in bed, her heart racing, and she listened.

She heard a gunshot.

That part had not been a dream.

She pulled on her pants, put on her shoes, and ran out into the morning. Joanna ran outside after her.

"It sounded like it came from the wash," Joanna said.

The two women ran down the wash, in the direction of the fence. Jack stood on this side of the fence with wire-cutters in his hand. The strands of barbed wire lay tangled on the right side, flung away from the site of the cut.

"Jack!" Maggie said. "Are you all right?"

He turned around when he heard her. She didn't see any blood on him. All was well.

"I'm fine," he said. "Some dingbat up in those hills is shooting at me."

"Gabriel!" Maggie shouted. "Is that you?"

"That's private property!" Gabriel yelled. "And he's destroying it."

"That's because it hurt this beautiful woman here," Jack shouted back. He looked around like he was trying to figure out just where the voice was coming from.

"Miss Doud told me to shoot any trespassers," Gabriel said.

"This is ridiculous," Maggie said. "Gabriel, someone is going to get hurt if you keep this up."

"He can't take down the fence!"

"You can't put a no trespassing sign in the middle of a river!" Maggie shouted.

"I'm gonna need to fix that fence now," Gabriel

said. "Is that crazy man gonna shoot me if I come down there?"

"We don't have any guns here," Maggie said.

"You shouldn't tell people that!" Gabriel yelled. "Now I could come rape and murder you in your sleep."

"Gabriel, I'm not going to keep yelling this conversation," Maggie said. "You can restring your stupid fence. No one will hurt you."

"I've got a wire-cutter," Jack said. "I could cut off his balls."

Maggie smacked Jack's arm.

"Come on," she said. "You've caused enough trouble."

"You ain't seen nothing yet," Jack said.

"I better have seen the last of this kind of shit," Maggie said. She grabbed the wire-cutters from him. "You could have gotten yourself killed. I don't think Gabriel is playing around."

The three of them started back toward the house.

"I'm not playing either," Jack said. "That fence hurt you. It had to pay."

"That is ridiculous," Maggie said. "I don't need rescuing, Jack. I don't want you doing anything like that again or I'm going to have to ask you to leave."

Jack stopped and looked at her.

She shook her head. "I'm serious, Jack. That's not the way I operate."

"I'm going home," Joanna said. "There's too much excitement around here for me."

"You don't want to stay and make some tinctures or essences?" Maggie asked.

Joanna shook her head.

 KIM ANTIEAU

"Suit yourself," Maggie said. "But we're here if you need us."

Maggie put the wire-cutters back in the barn.

"Jack, I'm going to go talk to Joan Doud," she said. "You want to come with me?"

"I thought you were mad at me?" he said.

"So what?" Maggie said. "Let's eat some breakfast and then go on up there. Why don't you get Anders. He's probably hungry."

"He was out all night again," Jack said, "so he's sleeping it off."

"Then you and I will eat breakfast," Maggie said. "And because you pissed me off so early in the morning, you can make that breakfast."

After they ate, Maggie and Jack went the long way around to get to Joan's house, just in case Gabriel was still out in the wash with a gun. As they topped the hill on Fifth Street, Maggie looked down at the rift. Some kind of roadwork equipment sat near the rift, but it was unmoving. The two police cars were still there, although now Maggie supposed she'd have to classify them as parked, rather than at the ready.

Jack and Maggie walked down Joan Doud's dirt drive. When they got to the house, Maggie knocked on Doud's front door.

"This is how we get things done in our neighborhood," Maggie said.

The door opened. Joan stood behind the metal door.

"May I help you?" she asked as though she had never seen Maggie before in her life.

"Joan, I would like you to reconsider the fence in the wash," Maggie said. "I was chasing after a dog last night and I forgot about the fence, and I ran right into it." She pulled up her sleeves to show Joan her cuts.

"I don't see anything," Joan said.

Maggie looked at her arm. She didn't see anything either. Not even a bruise. She pulled up her other sleeve. Nothing. Pulled the top of her shirt down so she could look at her chest. It was all healed.

"I saw it," Jack said. "She was bleeding and everything. It was traumatizing for all of us."

Maggie looked over at Jack. Traumatizing?

"It was," he said.

"Who is this person?" Joan asked.

"I'm the person who almost got shot today by—"

Maggie put her hand up. "Jack," she warned.

She turned and smiled at Joan. "This is my friend Jack. I told him that we solve our differences in this neighborhood with kindness and without violence."

"I know that I own this land," Joan said, "and strange things have been happening in that wash and I don't want them spilling up this hill into my yard and home. I don't want any strangers in the wash."

"I'm not a stranger," Maggie said. "I've lived here longer than you have!"

"What's that supposed to mean?"

"It means that I've lived here longer than you have," Maggie said. "We've always shared the wash."

"Not any more," Joan said. "I keep seeing some naked guy walking around in that wash at night. I've told Gabriel he has permission to shoot and I think the law would back me up on that."

"We're neighbors, Joan," Maggie said.

"Remember what they say," Joan said. "Fences make good neighbors."

    KIM ANTIEAU

Joan shut the door. Maggie made a noise. "I have no idea what that means!"

"Inanimate objects make better friends than real people," Jack said.

Maggie turned around and walked down the drive, away from the house.

"By the way, Mags," Jack said, "thanks for showing me how you get things done in this neighborhood."

Maggie looked at him. He grinned.

"Grrrr," she said.

NEXT

Late in the day, the electricity winked off again. Maggie didn't notice right away. She, Jack, and Anders sat on the bunkhouse porch watching the desert, pointing out this jackrabbit or that cardinal or a puffy white cloud floating by.

It all seemed so peaceful.

But then Anders said it felt nicer, as though a switch had been flipped. Maggie got up, opened the door to the bunkhouse, and leaned in to switch on the porch light—just to check. Nothing happened.

"Here we go again," she said.

She went into the barn and got her bike.

"You want company?" Jack asked. "I could see more examples of how you get things done around here."

"You're a funny guy," Maggie said.

"He is funny," Anders said. "I laugh all the time."

Maggie rode down to the rift. Huge earth-moving equipment was parked near the rift but nothing was happening. She rode right up to the edge and looked down. She could see things in the rift now. Before it had looked like an abyss. Now she saw an iron. Toaster oven. Bag of golf clubs. A golf cart.

"What is this?" she said.

"People are dumping their trash into the rift."

Maggie looked up. Shaw was there, with his clipboard.

"Who's doing that?"

He shook his head. "We don't know. We haven't seen anyone."

"But you're here all of the time," Maggie said.

He shrugged.

"I thought you were going to repair the road," Maggie said.

"They're having equipment trouble."

The man lied like he breathed.

"And the electricity," Maggie said. "What's up with that?"

"Another transformer blew."

"What do you need from us?" Maggie asked.

"Not everyone is accounted for," he said. "Either that or one of your neighbors is a terrorist."

Maggie sighed. "Everyone is accounted for in our neighborhood," Maggie said. "And if someone is a terrorist, we don't know about it."

"I'm sure you'd know," he said. "They'd be the ones talking about how incompetent the government is or about how this government has caused problems overseas. Or they might have maps in their house of the area. Or photographs of other countries."

Maggie laughed. He couldn't be serious.

"That would be just about everyone," Maggie said.

Shaw started to write something on his clipboard.

"I am joking!" Maggie said. "Stop writing! No one around here is especially anti-government."

"Especially?"

Oh shit. Why was she talking to this man at all?

Because he was on the other side of the rift. Where everyone wanted to be.

"No one here is anti-government," Maggie said. "We are all frustrated that this is taking so long. People may lose their jobs."

"They may lose more than that if we don't figure out what caused this rift," Shaw said.

"What does that mean?" Maggie asked. "Where are the scientists? Where are the investigators? They're the ones who can figure this out."

"We're a bit short-staffed in that area," he said.

He looked away from her. Was that what he did when he actually told the truth? Was that his "tell?"

"Can't you please do something about the electricity?" Maggie said. "I promise that we are telling you everything we know. But without electricity, our food supplies will spoil. Some of us can't eat the food you're dropping."

"What's wrong with the food?"

"None of it is fresh," Maggie said. "It's not whole food. It consists of cheese, milk powder, and white bread. Who eats that way?"

"Many people," he said. "And we're at war, remember."

"At war? What are you talking about?"

"Our country is at war on many fronts, especially here on the home front where we must be diligent about terrorists. We have no idea what was let loose here when the rift occurred.”

Maggie wanted to scream. She wondered if Shaw had ever read *Animal Farm, 1984,* or *Alas, Babylon.*

“I had a friend check to see if there was any radiation,” she said. “And there wasn’t any.”

Shaw just looked at her.

“So there’s nothing I can do for you and nothing you will do for us?” Maggie said. “Is that pretty much the situation?”

“We’re doing all we can at this time,” Shaw said.

Maggie got on her bike and rode away. She thought about going up to see Joanna, who seemed more stressed out than the rest of them. Maybe because her loved one was on the other side of the rift. Maybe because she didn’t have any work.

Instead, she rode up to Tilly’s house. The gate creaked open before she pressed the buzzer. Bill came out of the house.

“She’s not doing well,” he said. “I think she was looking forward to leaving and when they wouldn’t take her, it knocked the wind out of her. I’ll be out at the barn if you need me.”

Maggie nodded and went into the house. Tilly lay on the couch, a quilt draped over her. She smiled when she saw Maggie and started to sit up.

“Don’t get up on account of me,” Maggie said. “I’ll just curl up at the end of the couch with you and put my hands on you.”

“Sounds good,” Tilly said.

Tilly bent her knees a bit and Maggie sat on the end of the couch. She patted her thighs and Tilly rested her feet on Maggie. Maggie closed her eyes, dropped roots into the ground, felt the energy of the earth flow up her, asked for all her guides to be with her, and then she placed her hands on Tilly's ankles.

"You staying warm enough without the heat?" Maggie asked.

"You know us," Tilly say, "we don't ever turn the heat on in the winter unless it gets below forty."

"I don't want you getting cold," Maggie said.

"I'm warm enough," Tilly said. "How are the communal dinners going?"

Maggie wasn't even sure where it was today.

"Oh, you know," Maggie said. "Good and bad."

"Lisa can be overbearing," Tilly said.

"And everyone else seems so ready just to give in," Maggie said.

"Give in to what?"

Maggie shrugged. What did she mean?

"Give in to the fear of it," Maggie said, "or comply with whatever they want us to do."

"What do they want us to do?"

"I don't know," Maggie said.

"Do you ever think about the angel of death?" Tilly asked.

"No, I don't think I do."

"I've been wondering if there is such a thing," Tilly said, "or if that's our name for a certain kind of energy in the world. But in any case, the job of the Angel of Death is to essentially kill people, right?"

"I suppose so," Maggie said.

"So does that mean the Angel of Death is a serial killer?" Tilly asked.

Maggie laughed. "I never thought of it that way before, but you've got a point."

Maggie heard aircraft overhead and loud voices. Tilly looked up.

"What is that?"

"I don't know," Maggie said. "I'll go find out."

She got up and hurried to the front door, opened it, and stepped outside. Bill was standing in the middle of his yard with his rifle raised. Above them three drones flew, broadcasting this message: "This is the federal government. Martial law has been declared in your area. You are now required to return to your homes while we conduct on overhead infrared count. You are required by law to return to your own homes and remain there until further notice. You have one hour to comply. This is the federal government. Martial law has been declared."

Bill took aim at one of the drones and pulled the trigger. The noise made Maggie jumped.

"Damn it, Bill," Maggie said. "You're being ridiculous. That bullet isn't going to hurt that drone and it's going to come back to Earth and maybe hurt someone here. Sometimes you are such an asshole."

He put the gun to his side and looked at her. "Yeah, well, you talk to plants."

"I'd rather be talking to plants than to you right now."

"Hey, you two." They both looked toward the door where Tilly stood watching them. Maggie was immediately embarrassed.

"Geez, I'm sorry, Tilly," Maggie said. "Bill, I shouldn't have said that. None of my business. Guess this is getting to me a bit."

"Apology accepted," Bill said.

"William," Tilly said.

"And I'm sorry, too," he said. "I guess. What am I sorry for, Tilly? She does talk to plants."

"You shouldn't be shooting at the sky, for chrissakes," Tilly said. "Someone could get hurt."

"Point taken," Bill said. "It's too cold out here. Go back inside."

Maggie went to Tilly and gave her a gentle hug. "I'll stop by tomorrow."

Maggie got on her bike and rode home. She felt strangely tired and defeated. The sound of the drones faded away. As she went down the dirt roads, she looked at the cacti, the creosote bushes, and the mesquite trees. What did the plants think of all of this? Or did they even notice? Was this a human drama that had nothing to do with their lives? A red hawk flew overhead. Maggie waved.

Anders and Jack were in the garden when she got back home. She watched them work, leaning her chin on the top of the adobe wall. A few days ago, the garden plants had been scrawny, barely alive; now they were flourishing. How was that possible? The men worked close to each other, talking quietly. Maggie wondered if they were speaking to one another or to the plants.

"Both," Anders said. The men looked over at Maggie.

"Did I say that out loud?" Maggie asked.

"We're talking to the plants and each other," Jack said. "How have you been?"

"I went to see Tilly," she said. "She didn't seem very strong. And Bill was shooting at the drones. Did you hear them?"

"The drones?" Jack asked. "Yes."

Anders smiled at her. She couldn't help but smile at him. He was so pretty.

Or innocent.

Otherworldly?

"Who is Tilly?" Anders asked.

"She is a friend of mine who is ill," Maggie said. "Anders, do you know why there is a rift in the earth?"

He frowned. "Aren't there many rifts?"

"The one here," she said. "Near us."

"No," he said. "I do not know why."

"People are throwing junk into it," Maggie said.

Jack stood and leaned on his hoe. "That seems odd."

"We will make this a desert forest," Anders said. "An edible desert forest. You'll see. You will."

"Okay," Maggie said. "But for now let's go indoors, before the infrared machines come. Or whatever they are. I'm worried they'll find you, Anders, and take you away."

"I will go away," he said. "At the end of it. But they won't hurt me. I promise that."

Maggie looked at Jack. He shrugged.

"If the electricity is back on," Jack said, "I can heat us up some canned soup. Mmm-mmm good."

Later they heard planes overhead. Or some kind of flying machinery. They didn't go out of doors to check. The three of them sat in Maggie's living room playing cards. Jack taught Anders how to play Crazy Eights, and he quite liked it.

"You've never played cards before?" Jack asked.

Anders shook his head.

"I guess if I could be invisible I wouldn't play cards either," Jack said.

"How does that possibly follow?" Maggie asked.

"I could follow you around, for one," Jack said. "And you'd never know."

"And that would be fun why?"

Anders yawned. He put his cards down and curled up on the couch. Reminded Maggie of a cat. He closed his eyes and was soon sleeping.

"Maybe it is time for bed," Maggie said.

Jack shrugged. "I could play a few more hands. Try gin this time?"

Maggie nodded. Jack gathered all the cards together and then shuffled the deck.

"Are you happy living out here?" Jack asked.

"I am," she said. "I guess. I moved here to get away from the city and my family. I felt like they were all in so much pain so much of the time and I couldn't do anything about it. So I moved out here. Started our business. I don't try to help anyone who doesn't want help. I feel like I do some good. For most of my life, I thought I wanted community, but once I was here, I didn't know what that meant—maybe because most people I meet don't really want to be in community. Or maybe I don't want to be in community with them."

Jack laughed. "Do you think we're the only species who despises our own?"

"Male lions kill baby lions," Maggie said. "So that the lioness will go into heat."

"Do they eat them once they kill them?" Jack asked.

"I don't know," Maggie said. She shuddered. "Something about that whole thing I find very disturbing. I mean, if it's all about evolution, how does killing lion cubs help preserve the species?"

"The lion is interested in preserving his line," Jack

said. "He probably doesn't care about the species in general."

"How do the lions know they aren't killing their own cubs? The ones they fathered?"

"I have no idea," Jack said, "since this is the first I ever heard of this. But maybe they can tell."

"How? How could they possible know?"

Jack shrugged. "Maybe they don't. Maybe they're just horny killers."

"Who started this conversation?"

"You did," he said. "We started to talk about you so you changed the topic to something gruesome."

"Something less gruesome than talking about myself," Maggie said. "I mean, really, at our age, who wants to talk about their lives? I moved out here looking for some magic. Living outside the mainstream of America ain't all it's cracked up to be. I should have thought it through more. I don't have any money. I don't have many friends. I'm the butt of too many jokes. All the men my age are either assholes or assholes looking for some young chicka."

"Wow," Jack said. "What category am I in?"

"I don't know you well enough to know," Maggie said. "I'm sorry. I shouldn't categorize people like that. What about you, Jack? Are you happy with your life?"

"I gotta say the last few days here with you and Anders have been the most peaceful time of my life," he said. "No one cares about who I am or who I'm not. My thirst for alcohol seems to have diminished some. I wouldn't mind if the rift went on forever. Although I do understand most people want and need to get on the other side of the rift. But for me, I kind of like being here."

Maggie squinted and peered at Jack.

"I appreciate you looking after Anders," Maggie said. "You are kind to him."

"I can see you care for him," he said.

"Is that why you're nice to him?"

"Naw," he said. "He's a fun guy. Not like most men I know who are either assholes or assholes looking for some young chicka."

Maggie laughed. "Come on. Less talking, more dealing."

NEXT

In the morning, the electricity was off again. Maggie ate dry cereal. Then she went out to the bunkhouse and Desert Bloomers. Neither Jack nor Anders were there.

Maggie got on her bike and went down to the rift. The road equipment was no longer parked near the rift. Maggie got off the bike and stood at the edge and looked down. More items had been thrown into the chasm. A three-wheeler was upside down on one of the ledges in the rift. Near it were toasters, microwave ovens, ironing boards, book cases.

"What is going on?" she said.

Jeff Shaw walked over to the edge of the rift on the other side.

"You are in violation of martial law," he said. "I could have you arrested."

Maggie looked at him. "Oh, so we're not even pretending to play nice any longer?" She shrugged. "Go ahead and arrest me." She held out her arms. "I'll wait until you bring over the cuffs."

"You're not taking this seriously," he said. "There has been a break. Between worlds. Between dimensions. Something. We're trying to plug it up. We're trying to find the cause. Maybe you were the cause. You and your friends. Or just you, wanting to be different. And now you are not helping."

"A break? Between *dimensions?* What are you talking about? Before it was terrorism. Before that it was an earthquake. In-between was radiation. You change your story every two minutes. You just want us to live in fear so we'll do exactly what you say. It worked. We've all done what you've told us to do. By the way, how are we supposed to get the food you're dropping for us if we can't leave our homes?"

Shaw held his clipboard close to his chest.

"Yesterday, people dumped half the food into the rift," he said. "Said it was garbage and people couldn't live on it. But people all over the world live on it. Beggars can't be choosers."

Maggie laughed. It must have been Lisa. She wished she had been there to see it.

"We need fresh fruit and vegetables," she said. "And if the electricity keeps going off, we're going to need water. Why don't you put some boards over the rift and let us come and go as we please? Then you all could just go home."

"This is bigger than that," Shaw said. "We will find who we are looking for. If you cooperate, things will go easier on you. If you don't, then it will be more difficult for you."

"I have no idea what you are talking about," Maggie

said. "We have done everything you asked. Please just fix the road, turn on our electricity, and let things get back to normal."

He began writing something on his clipboard. Maggie made a noise and turned away from him. She got on her bike and rode away. She realized she didn't really care if they fixed the road. The only thing on the other side of the road were her clients—and food, she supposed. But she didn't like feeling trapped here and she definitely wanted electricity and running water.

She stopped by Nina and John's house, but no one answered the door when she knocked.

She rode over to Lisa and Ricardo's house. No one answered there either, so she tried the doorknob.

The door was locked. She had never been to their home when the door was locked. She pressed the doorbell.

After another minute, the door opened. Lisa stood on the other side of the screen door, shotgun in hand.

"Hello to you, too," Maggie said.

Lisa looked around. "What are you doing here?"

"I came to see how you're doing," she said.

"We're fine," she said.

"Can I come in?"

"No," Lisa said. "We're not supposed to leave our homes. What? Are you stupid?"

"You're asking me that when you're standing there holding a gun on your friend and neighbor?"

"I gotta protect my family," she said. "Go home. No telling what's coming next."

She shut the door. Maggie stood staring at the closed door for a moment, dumbfounded. How could things have changed so quickly and so drastically?

Maggie got back on her bike and rode home.

Anders and Jack were sitting on the bunkhouse porch, staring at the Catalina Mountains in the distance.

"Next time you two leave in the middle of the day, could you leave a note or something?" Maggie said. The two men looked at each other and then at her.

"Sure," Jack said. "Didn't mean to alarm you."

Maggie turned away from them and went into Desert Bloomers. She phoned Joanna. No one answered. She left a message: "Let me know you're okay please." She hung up. Then she decided to call Tilly. She picked up the phone again. This time there was no dial tone, just a woman's automated voice saying, "The telephone company is aware of the problem and will fix it soon. The telephone company is aware of the problem and will fix it soon. Please call us if you have any questions. The telephone company . . ."

"How can we call you when the phones don't work?" Maggie slammed the phone down.

"Is everything okay?" Jack stood in the doorway.

"No," she said. "Jeff Shaw threatened to arrest me, and Lisa threatened to shoot me. It's not shaping up to be a very good day."

"But the sun is out and the sky is blue," Jack said. "We've got some food left and Anders and I filled up every jug, jar, and bucket with water before the electricity went out again."

"You mean it came back on?"

"For a few minutes."

"Where were you?"

"We were right here," Jack said. "Anders was teaching me to be invisible."

"I guess it worked," Maggie said, "because I didn't see you."

"We're going to have a fire later," Jack said. "Gonna cook some prickly pear. And whatever else is gonna go bad in the fridge. Sound good?"

"Sure," Maggie said. "I'm going to check on Tilly and Joanna. I'll be back for a late lunch or early dinner."

"Your men will be waiting for you," he said.

"I appreciate it," she said. "We should be able to get food from the garden soon, too, by the looks of it. Anders has the greenest thumb I've ever seen. I do believe he must be magic."

"Must be," Jack said.

Maggie left Desert Bloomers and got on her bike again. She headed over to Tilly and Bill's house. She found them both sitting on their back porch drinking tea and looking out at the Rincon Mountains.

Tilly stood to greet her. She looked strong and healthy today. Her cheeks were red.

"Sit," Tilly said. "Bill, can you go get her a cup?"

"Oh no, I'm fine," Maggie said. She sat next to Bill.

"I'll get you a cup," Bill said. "That'll give you ladies time to chitchat."

Bill got up and went into the house. Maggie could hear his cowboy boots click-clacking on the hardwood floor.

"You look great," Maggie said. "You're feeling well?"

"I am," Tilly said. "The most amazing thing happened last night. This very white man came to see me. He was so white he was nearly glowing. I thought maybe he was Jesus or something but he was naked. It's difficult to imagine Jesus walking around naked. Especially since it was so cold last night."

"Was this in a dream?" Maggie asked, although she suspected Tilly had seen Anders wandering the 'hood.

"No, I was wide awake," she said. "He knocked on the sliding glass window. I don't know why I opened it. I could see he was naked. Naked and glowing. He wanted to make certain I wasn't afraid. He said he had gone into another house looking for me and the woman got very scared. I told him I wasn't afraid."

"So what happened?"

"He came in and sat with me," she said. "We talked. I don't even know what we talked about. I think he held my hand. It felt like I was holding an electrical current, only it didn't hurt. I think I fell to sleep because when I woke up, it was morning, and I was on the couch and the man was gone. And I felt better than I've felt in years."

Maggie smiled. "I'm so glad," she said. "What a wonderful gift."

"Joan Doud came over a few days ago and warned us about some naked man wandering the wash," Tilly said. "It must be the same man, but I don't think he means anyone any harm. He says clothes just hurt him."

Maggie nodded.

She suddenly felt an urge to check on Joan Doud.

"I think this is really good," Maggie said, "but I just remembered I forgot to do something. I'll come by tomorrow."

Bill came back onto the porch carrying a cup.

"Sorry, Bill, got to run."

Tilly reached her hand up to her. "I'm ready for a new adventure, Maggie. I think I know what the dream meant the other night, about crossing to the other side. Thanks for everything."

Maggie took Tilly's hand and squeezed it. Then she kissed her cheek. She hugged Bill too.

Then she hurried out of the house, got on her bike, and pedaled over to Joan Doud's house. She let the bike drop to the ground and she went to the front door and knocked.

No one answered.

She rang the bell.

Still no one came.

"Joan! Gabriel!"

She went around to the back door. She pounded on it. No one answered.

She tried the door handle. It moved easily. She opened the door and went inside. She stood on the threshold for a moment, waiting for her eyes to adjust to the darkness.

"Joan!" she called.

She went into the living room. It was empty.

She went down the hallway to Joan's bedroom.

Joan lay in bed, dressed in her pajamas. Her eyes were wide open.

"Joan?"

She didn't move.

Maggie went to her side. She took her wrist in her hand. Joan was cold. Maggie felt for her pulses on both wrists anyway.

She didn't have any. Pulses.

"Oh crap," Maggie said.

Had Anders done this?

Maggie left the room and the house. She went out to

the barn where Gabriel sat outside the bunkhouse smoking a cigarette. He looked up at her.

"We're not supposed to leave the house," he said.

"She's dead," Maggie said. "When did it happen?"

Gabriel stubbed the cigarette out in the dirt. Then he put the stub in his breast pocket. "She cannot stand seeing cigarette butts anywhere," he said. "I heard her scream last night or early this morning. But I didn't go in. I often hear her scream and it turns out to be a spider or mouse or a bad dream. I was tired. I didn't feel like going in. She's like a child. I should have gone, though, because now she's dead."

"There was nothing you could have done," Maggie said. Although she didn't have a clue if he could have done anything or not. "It looks like she died of natural causes." She hoped she had died of natural causes. Was being scared to death a natural cause?

"Did you call and tell anyone?" Maggie asked.

"The phones don't work," he said, "and the flying machines said we weren't to leave here. I am ready to leave. I miss my wife and my children."

"I'll go down to the rift and tell them," she said.

"You want I take down the fence now?" he asked.

Maggie shook her head. "No, the fence is the least of our worries now."

Maggie left Gabriel alone. She went around to the front of the house and got her bike. She started riding toward the rift, but just then she saw military tanks and people dressed in riot gear carrying guns coming across the rift, traveling over what looked like a kind of temporary wooden bridge.

A drone flew overhead announcing, "We are here to protect you. We are looking for intruders. Keep your

   KIM ANTIEAU

doors open or we will break them down. We are here to protect you. We are looking for intruders . . ."

"Oh Christ," Maggie said. She turned the bike around and headed toward home. They must be looking for Anders. She dropped the bike into the dirt at the head of the wash. She didn't have time to ride the long way home. She dipped into the wash and began running, her feet slip-sliding on the sand. Maybe they could hide Anders in the barn.

Or something.

The sand hardened into dirt for a stretch and Maggie was able to run. She came to the place where she had first seen the blue-black horse and then Anders. She took a deep breath, couldn't help it, something different about the spot. Then she was at the wire fence. She ducked under it and ran home.

It was too late. The men in black riot gear were already there. Must have crossed the rift over where Shaw was, too. Jack was standing off to the side as the men— and women?—streamed into her house.

Maggie ran after them. She tried to push past them into her house.

"You have no right!" she called. "How can you do this? This could happen to any of you, anywhere. We have done nothing wrong!"

One of the riot police pushed her out of the way. She couldn't see his face. He could have been a robot for all she knew. Jack pulled her away, out of the house. She looked at him, trying to suss out whether Anders was safe or not. They had to protect Anders. They had to protect him from this.

After a few minutes, the riot police marched out of

the house. Then they went through the barn—through the horse stalls, the bunkhouse, and Desert Bloomers.

Then they marched away.

The day was preternaturally quiet again.

When Maggie was certain they were gone and out of earshot, she hurried into the house.

"Where is he?" she asked, turning around in her living room. "Anders?"

And suddenly she saw him. It was as if he was not there and then he was. Or as if he had stepped away from the wall which had been camouflaging him.

He walked up to Maggie and embraced her.

"You mustn't worry about me," he said. "You do not need to protect or save me."

Maggie put her arms around him. "You don't know how hard they can be."

Anders gently pulled away from her. He took her hand. "Come," he said, "you can watch while Coyote Jack and I make fire."

Jack laughed. "Yep, we're gonna rub two sticks together until we create a regular conflagration."

"Wait," Maggie said. "Jack, we'll meet you outside."

Jack looked at her quizzically. Then he said, "All right. I'll be awaitin'."

Jack left the house. Maggie looked into Anders's eyes.

"Anders, I went over to Joan Doud's house," she said. "Do you know who that is?"

Anders nodded. "I don't understand this place. There is so much fear. I was invited here, but everyone is so afraid."

"Who invited you here?"

"Don't you know?" Anders asked.

Maggie shook her head. "Anders, I need to know if you hurt her. You can't hurt people."

"I went to the wrong place," he said. "I thought she was calling for me. But when I went into the house, she was afraid. And then she disappeared."

"But you didn't touch her," Maggie said. "Or put a spell on her or anything?"

"I did not touch her," Anders said. "And I do not know how to spell her."

Maggie laughed. She knew she shouldn't. She knew it was awful that Joan was dead. She didn't want her dead. She put her hand over her mouth to stop the laugh.

Then she wanted to sob.

Poor Joan. Afraid of everything.

"Anders," Maggie said, "don't tell anyone that you saw Joan. This is something we should just keep between us."

Anders nodded. "Will other people disappear like she did? She left her clothes behind. I couldn't tell where she went."

"That's too bad," Maggie said. "I think a lot of people would like to know where she went. Wherever everyone goes once they . . . leave their clothes behind."

For the next few days, Maggie felt like things calmed down, or at least the three of them fell into a kind of rhythm—or routine. The temporary bridges over the rift were removed. The drones went over three times a day, demanding that any nonresidents report to the rift; all area residents were ordered to stay at home except when retrieving food from the drop off point near the rift. The electricity stayed off.

Gabriel stopped by once to tell her the riot police had sent someone out to take away Joan's body. He was still staying in the bunkhouse, although he went into the house sometimes to scrounge for food. Maggie told him he was welcome to visit them any time.

Jack and Maggie went up to Joanna's house. At first she didn't answer the door. But Maggie kept pounding on it. Eventually she opened it and let them in. She looked ill or afraid or both.

"I miss Alex so much I can hardly stand it," she told them. "And I haven't been able to reach her for days."

"You can't stay holed up here," Maggie said. "What are you eating?"

"Alex was prepared for everything," Joanna said. "I've got enough canned goods to last weeks. And we've got so much water. Plus I've got a generator."

"You never said," Maggie said.

"Alex told me to keep it a secret," she said. "We had to look out after ourselves."

"I don't know if everyone in the neighborhood has enough water," Maggie said. "We're going to run out soon."

Joanna nodded. "I know I should be a better person. But I don't want to run out."

Maggie hugged her friend.

"You gotta do what you gotta do," she said. "But you're welcome to come stay with me."

Maggie and Jack decided that since they had no electricity and therefore no plumbing, they would need a latrine. So Anders, Jack, and Maggie began digging one. Anders laughed and sang most of the time. Maggie watched his muscles ripple beneath her purple blouse as he dug and she wished again that he would wear a T-shirt—for her viewing enjoyment if nothing else.

Two of their neighbors—Laurel Smith and Daniel Vess—came over and helped. They barely said a word, besides hello; they just started digging.

One evening Jack and Anders started a fire to roast piñon nuts and prickly pear pads. Laurel and Daniel came over with some dried fruits and vegetables. They also brought over a sun oven and proposed they all try to make lunch the next day on it. John and Nina wandered over, too, carrying a salad they had made from some canned vegetables.

Tilly continued to improve. One day, when they were experimenting with the sun oven, Tilly and Bill rode their horses over to Maggie's place. Bill laid two skinned and gutted rabbits on Maggie's picnic table.

"I said all the necessary prayers before I killed them," Bill said.

Maggie looked at him. "I didn't know you prayed."

He nodded. "I pray to the wind. To the sun. To these animals who sacrificed themselves for us."

Anders came up to the table and looked at the rabbits. He began to cry. Then he sobbed. Maggie put her arms across his shoulders. "We don't have to eat them," she said. "Bill can take them away."

"No," he said. "Then their deaths would be meaningless. We should celebrate their lives." He leaned over and kissed Bill on the cheek. "Thank you." Then he stepped off the bunkhouse porch and headed for the fire pit which Jack was preparing along with Laurel and Nina. Daniel and John were in the desert looking for wood to burn.

Bill looked at Maggie as if to say, "One of yours, I presume?"

"Thanks, Bill," she said.

He smiled and shook his head.

Tilly came up on the porch and sat in one of the chairs in the shade of the overhang.

"Is that your naked white man?" Maggie asked.

"I don't want to know," Bill said. He picked up the rabbits and jumped off the porch and headed for the fire pit.

"I believe it is," Tilly said. "Although it seems like a dream now."

"It was real," Maggie said. "You're real. He's real. And the healing is real."

"You heard that Joan Doud died," Tilly said.

"I did," Maggie said.

"That's where you went that day after I told you about the naked white man, isn't it? You knew she was dead."

"No, I didn't know until I got there."

"You think he did it?" Tilly said. "What's his name?"

"Anders," Maggie said.

"You think Anders killed her?"

Maggie shook her head. "No, I don't, Tilly. Joan Doud killed herself with her fear."

Tilly nodded. "That is what I believe, too."

They were silent for a few moments.

"We're going to have to decide soon," Tilly said. "Whether we go to the other side of the rift or not. I think I know what we'll do. But what about you, Maggie? Have you decided what life you want?"

Maggie looked over at her. "I thought I decided that

a long time ago," she said. "But now I think maybe I've been waffling all of these years. I'm not sure I've really believed in what I've been doing all this time. Part of me wondered if everyone was right: Maybe I am just a crazy lady who talks to plants."

"Isn't crazy in the eye of the beholder?" Tilly asked. "I behold you, and I don't believe you are crazy. But I do think sometimes we have to decide. We have to commit to our life."

"I've never been very good with commitments," Maggie said.

Tilly laughed. "Yes, you are! You commit to every person you work with. When it's time, you'll know what you want."

"I may not have a choice," Maggie said. "Shaw and his people are trying to make the choice for us."

"Then we shouldn't let them," Tilly said. "We should do something. Something unexpected. They think we're sheep. Maybe we should show them that we're sheep with teeth. Or at least wolves with a strange fashion sense."

Maggie laughed.

That night many of their neighbors showed up, lured out of their homes by the sight of a fire or the smell of food. Joanna rode down from her place with Boxer and Crazy Lu, carrying multiple gallon jugs of water. Those who needed water took some; others promised to distribute them to people they knew were in need.

The group of neighbors and friends ate together and told stories around the fire. They didn't talk about the rift or the reason for it.

When the moon rose in the sky that evening, they all howled their gratitude.

In the morning, before the sun was up, Maggie stood in the driveway in her bare feet. She held a rattle in one hand. She began to shake it. Then she began to sing.

"Up, Sun, up! We love and need you! Up, Sun, up! We sing to you in deep love and gratitude! Up, Sun, up!" She did a little dance in the sand.

Joanna wandered out of the house, wiping dreams from her eyes, and she went into Desert Bloomers—where Anders lived—and got a rattle. Soon Joanna and Maggie were rattling and dancing. Jack and Anders came out of their respective rooms. They danced and sang, too. Sunlight peeked out and over the Rincon Mountains, plating the landscape temporarily with gold.

The group hooted and hollered.

"Thank you, Sun!"

   KIM ANTIEAU

NEXT

The neighbors continued to gather at Maggie's house to cook. The sun ovens worked perfectly. Maggie wondered why she hadn't used them before. She and Joanna began ferrying water to those neighbors who needed it. Some had stocked up; some had generators. Some still went down to the rift and got their supplies from there, although fewer and fewer people went to the rift.

Gabriel often came down the wash to spend the day with them.

Jack and Anders helped neighbors build latrines and get their gardens started. As much as they could, people ignored the rift and the daily drones telling them to stay in their homes and turn over any intruders.

Every morning, Maggie and the others prayed and rattled for the sun to come up. And every morning, more people gathered than had the day before.

Every evening, people came together to eat and talk.

Some of them hunted and brought meat to the table. Others went out wildcrafting for desert edibles.

Then Joanna's generator ran out of gas and the solar panel on her pump stopped working. When Jack and Maggie went to examine at it, the solar panel appeared damaged, as if someone had tried and succeeded in breaking it.

They would run out of water soon and be forced to use what they were dropping at the rift.

One night after everyone had gone back to their homes, Jack sat with Maggie on the back porch of the bunkhouse. Anders had left earlier to wander the wash. And crows gathered in the cottonwoods and mesquite trees. Maggie had never seen so many crows in mesquite trees before, but now they were here, there, and everywhere.

"Maggie," Jack said. "I'm afraid this isn't going to last. It's just a reprieve until it gets bad."

Maggie nodded. "It's been nice though," she said. "For the first time I felt as though I was part of something. I hope Ricardo and Alicia are all right."

"Ricardo can take care of his family," Jack said. "They'll be fine. Mags, do you want to go over the rift?"

Maggie squinted into the darkness. "I don't know what you mean."

"If you had a choice," he said, "right now, would you go across the rift, to the other side?"

She shook her head. "No. It's too late for me. I've lived this life for too long. And that life—the one across the rift—is a life I left behind a long time ago." She slapped her thighs. "I should go see what Jeff Shaw and company has planned for us. I haven't been down there in days."

"You know, it's almost over," Jack said. "Another eclipse is coming. It will all change again. If you want Anders, you should go to him now."

Maggie looked over at Jack. "What do you mean?"

"He's going to be gone soon," Jack said. "If you want him, you should just go up to him and give him a big kiss. Or whatever. Tell him you want to trip the light fantastic with him."

Maggie laughed. "He's like a child, Jack."

"He isn't," Jack said. "He's a man. Or man-like, at least. I'm sure he could perform his manly duties. I've seen him naked."

Maggie leaned back and laughed.

"I'm serious," Jack said.

"I see that you are, CJ," Maggie said. "But I haven't any yearnin' that way."

"I've seen the way you look at him," Jack said.

"I look at him the way I look at a sunset," Maggie said, "or the way I look at a beautiful flower or a wild river. I love them all, but it doesn't mean I want to fuck them."

Jack frowned.

"So those aren't your bedroom eyes?"

Maggie laughed so hard she began crying.

"What kind of women have you spent your life around anyway?" Maggie said. "No, don't answer that. I appreciate you looking out for me, Jack, but I told you you don't have to rescue me or fix me. You can be my friend. I don't have too many of those."

"Is that what you think?" Jack asked. "You have no idea. Why do you think all of these people have been coming here? It's because of you, Mags. They love and admire you. They feel safe with you."

Maggie shook her head. "I don't know why. I have no idea what I'm doing."

"Join the rest of the human race," Jack said.

Maggie stood. She leaned over and kissed the top of Jack's head.

"You're a good man, Coyote Jack," she said.

She walked across the wash, down the dirt road, and then out to Speedway, and headed toward the black slash in the ground.

Jeff Shaw was standing at the rift when she got to it.

"You haven't turned over the intruder," Shaw said.

"Because there is no intruder," Maggie said. "It's just us. You sent your storm troopers in. They didn't find anything or anyone. No sign of terrorism."

"I wouldn't go that far," he said. "And since you are not cooperating, we will be taking drastic measures."

"How aren't we cooperating?"

"You aren't staying in your homes," he said. "You are not lining up for food in an orderly fashion."

"We aren't staying in our homes because we have to eat and get water," Maggie said.

"We have been providing plenty of food and water," he said.

"You have been providing us with swill while trying to terrorize us with drones, with riot police, with infra-red scans. Fix the goddamn road and let us go! You've imprisoned us without reason or cause. That is against the rules of our particular country."

"We are going to build a wall," Shaw said, "to prevent anyone from escaping. And then we may or may not dust the area."

   KIM ANTIEAU

"Dust the area? What does that mean?"

"We'll use a gas to put you all to sleep," he said. "Then we can come onto your side safely and assess the situation."

"What?" Maggie said. "You're going to *gas* us? Are you crazy? We're U.S. citizens. You can't gas us or wall us in just because we happen to be on the so-called wrong side of a line in the earth."

"We can and we will," he said. "You have a choice. If you turn over any intruders, if you tell us what happened to cause the rift, then we'll negotiate an end to this."

"Negotiate?" Maggie said. "We're not at war."

"We know that you've been burning fires," he said, "and hunting and growing gardens. It seems as though you have all been prepared for this. Maybe even planned it."

Maggie stared at him. "I cannot believe this," she said. She closed her eyes.

Breathe, breathe. Help me. Someone help me.

Maybe this is all a dream, a dream.

She saw in her mind's eye the great saguaro standing tall and steady, slowly dancing through the year, as though it had all the time in the world.

Time. Yes, time.

Thank you, Saguaro.

She could hear the paloverde breathing. She remembered how the paloverde had looked almost silver in the moonlight. The eclipse. Anders said it would be over after the eclipse. Hadn't he? Or at least he would be gone then. Maybe everything would go back to normal after he left.

Thank you, Paloverde.

"All right," Maggie said. "You win. I will try to use

my influence—what little I have—to discover if anyone is hiding anything. But it will take some time. People are afraid and are hiding in their homes, most of them with guns. This is a situation that needs some finesse, not bullying. Can you give me a few days?"

"How many?"

When was the New Moon? Two nights? Two nights until the eclipse?

"Five days," Maggie said.

"I'll give you two," he said. "Day after tomorrow we start."

"Four," Maggie said.

"I'm not bargaining with you," he said. "Day after tomorrow we're bringing in the big guns."

Whatever that meant.

Maggie headed back toward her house. What could they do in two days? Hang on for dear life and hope Anders got away, if that's who they were looking for. Hope things would return to normal?

But what if that didn't happen? Or what if they really did gas them and build a fence, no matter what.

Jack was waiting for Maggie when she returned. She stood in the middle of the drive, in the darkness, and said quietly to him, "Day after tomorrow, they say they're going to build a wall to keep us in and gas us so they can come in and find out what's going on here."

He shook his head. "Man, that's what someone with a short wave radio told me. What they're hearing on the other side isn't good. They're calling us all traitors. They're saying we're not even U.S. citizens, but even if we are, we're terrorists so we have no rights."

"Why didn't you tell me this before? Why didn't you tell all of us this before?"

   KIM ANTIEAU

"It just sounded so paranoid," he said. "I thought it was all bullshit. Come on. This is Arizona. There are a lot of nuts and nutty conspiracy theories out there. But now. Sounds like serious business."

"We've got to figure out a way to get over the rift," she said.

"I agree," Jack said. "I've been doing some recon and I found a place a little south of here, just out of another wash where the cholla and mesquite grow close together. The rift isn't as wide there and there aren't any police right there. I think we could throw a long board across there and just walk across."

"Do we have a board long enough in the barn?" Maggie asked.

"Gabriel and I could rustle something up. We'd have to be discreet, maybe nail it together once we got to the place."

Maggie nodded. "We don't know who we can trust," Maggie said. "We might tell someone and then they rat us out. But we can't just go over ourselves and leave everyone here. I mean, if they're really going to build a wall and gas people, we've got to warn people."

"I agree," Jack said.

"I told Shaw I'd go around and talk to everyone," Maggie said. "See if I can find out anything. I was just stalling for time. But if the drones see me out and about, that's what they'll think I'm doing. Instead, I could tell people what's happening and we could arrange for them to meet here and we could take them to the narrow place in the rift."

"We'd have to time the trips to the rift in-between drone pass overs," Jack said.

Maggie nodded. Fortunately, they went over fairly regularly: morning, noon, and early evening.

"I know we can trust Bill and Tilly," Maggie said. "We'll tell them first. Crack of dawn, let's start doing this."

Jack nodded. "You got it, Mags."

Maggie went into her house and told Joanna what Shaw had told her.

"We need to leave here," Maggie said. "And we need to get everyone else out. If they're willing."

"Thank god," Joanna said. "I am all in."

Maggie awakened just before dawn. She went out and sang up the dawn with many of her neighbors. When the sun was up, she turned to them and told them what Shaw had said about the wall and the gas. She watched their terrified faces. For a moment, it felt as though the whole world was filled with fear. It vibrated around them.

"Jack and I have a plan," Maggie said, "to get us all over to the other side. We'll need your help and your discretion."

They gathered around Maggie and Jack and made plans. They would make three trips: one mid-morning, one mid-afternoon, and one early evening.

"I think we should tell everyone," Maggie said, "even if it puts us at risk."

Nina said, "What if someone reports us? Then none of us will get out."

"We can decide now, as a group," Maggie said.

"I just want to get back to Alexandria," Joanna said. "Honestly, I don't care about all those people hiding in their homes, waiting to be saved, willing to hurt others."

Some in the group murmured their approval.

"We've all been afraid," Maggie said.

"Didn't you keep the existence of your generator a secret for a while?" John asked Joanna. "We've all done things because we've been afraid. None of us has done anything to deserve being imprisoned here. Certainly none of us has done anything worthy of being gassed."

"Do you think they meant it?" Nina asked. "I mean, maybe they're just threatening us, trying to see how we'd respond."

"Maybe it's all some kind of experiment," Jack said. "And we're the guinea pigs. We just don't know. I know it's time to get out of Dodge and we're offering a way out. Now we need to decide if we tell everyone or we just go on our own."

"Let's vote," Laurel said.

Maggie nodded. "All in favor of telling our neighbors about our escape plan, raise your hands."

Most everyone raised a hand.

"All in favor of not telling anyone else."

No one raised a hand.

Power of peer pressure, Maggie thought.

"Okay," Maggie said. "Tell your neighbors. Tell them the time and the place. Don't bring anything but a backpack. In case they're tracking us some other way, we just want to look like we're out for a hike."

The group dispersed. Jack and Gabriel went to make the wooden "bridge." Maggie looked for Anders, but he wasn't in Desert Bloomers or in the garden.

She and Joanna went out on the horses to tell the rest of the neighbors about their escape plan. Some people answered their doors; some stayed hidden inside. Once or twice, Maggie pounded on front and back doors. She knew people were inside. She felt nearly desperate to tell them what might happen soon.

She felt she had to do something to save them.

"Maggie," Joanna finally said. "We need to get back soon. We've told who we can tell. Now let's go."

They arrived back at Maggie's house just after the first drone had gone overhead. Maggie's driveway was filled with people.

Jack carried a long board over his shoulder. Gabriel stood next to him with another board slung over his shoulder. He also held a pair of pruning scissors.

"That is not very discreet," Maggie said. "I hope they don't see you."

"I've got the way figured out," Jack said. "We won't be in view of the police. Maybe from the overhead police, but we'll have to risk it."

"What are the shears for?" Maggie said.

"To make a path to the rift," Jack said, "so we can get in and out more quickly. It's pretty overgrown."

"Okay," Maggie said, "but make sure you ask permission of the plants first. Ask them to pull their energy back from their limbs before you cut them."

"Got it, Mags."

"So you really do talk to plants?" Gabriel asked.

"I really do," she said.

Tilly and Bill made their way through the crowd to Maggie. Tilly and Maggie hugged. Bill looked positively ecstatic.

"You coming?" Tilly asked.

Maggie shook her head. "I want to try and tell more of our neighbors."

Plus she wanted to find Anders.

"I think good things are coming," Tilly said.

Maggie nodded. "Yes!" she said. "I'm glad you're able to go."

"Have you decided if you're going to cross the rift at all?" Tilly asked.

"I'm certainly not going to stay here and wait for them to decide my destiny," Maggie said.

Tilly nodded. "Good," she said. "Will I ever see you again?"

"Sure," Maggie said. She kissed Tilly again. She felt butterflies in her stomach.

She probably wouldn't see her again.

"We need to get going," Jack said. "Try to be invisible, people!"

Maggie smiled. Jack looked over at her.

"I should have had Anders teach us how," he said.

"Where is he?" Maggie asked.

"I don't know," he said. "Wish us luck."

"Luck," Maggie said. "You coming back?"

"Sure," he said. "I've got two more groups to lead. I'll see you for lunch."

Maggie watched the group form a long single file.

"May you all be safe, may you be safe, you are safe," Maggie whispered.

Joanna came and stood next to her. Maggie put her arm across her shoulder.

"I thought you were leaving," Maggie said.

Joanna shrugged.

"Figured we could go tell some of our other neighbors," she said. "Further up. Then I'll go."

Maggie and Joanna rode east a bit and informed more of their neighbors. Maggie knew it was a risk every time they told one more person. She wished Joanna had left with the others. She didn't like jeopardizing her freedom.

Before noon, they returned to Maggie's house. Jack was sitting on the bunkhouse porch, waiting. The second group of escapees hadn't gathered yet.

Jack smiled and stood up when he saw them.

"It worked, Mags," Jack said. "We did it. Gabriel, John, Nina, Tilly, and Bill all got across. That reminds me."

Jack kissed Maggie on the mouth.

"What was that for?" she asked.

"Tilly said to give you a kiss for her," Jack said.

"Gotta tell you, Jack. Tilly and I never kissed on the mouth."

Jack shook his head. "Her loss," he said. "And maybe yours, too."

Maggie laughed.

Just then, they heard the drones flying over.

"Let's get something to eat," Joanna said. "I want to have my strength up for when I see my sweetheart again!"

Maggie went with the second group. Jack led them expertly through the desert brush. Joanna and Maggie stayed at the rear of the group, watching out for stragglers—and storm troopers. She kept waiting for them to be caught, for something horrible to happen. Yet at the same time, she felt they were protected and hidden by the desert as they walked on the path, passing by mesquite, cholla, prickly pear, paloverde, and various other desert brush. Every once in a while, a rabbit ran across the path or a small bird fluttered just above them.

For the most part, no one said anything.

   KIM ANTIEAU

Then, unexpectedly, they were at the rift. It was no-
ticeably narrower here.

Why hadn't they looked for this kind of escape earlier?

Were they so used to being told what to do?

She should have looked. She should have known.
She was the one who lived on the margins. She was
the witch in the cottage at the edge of the village. She
should have looked.

She shook her head.

It was time for her to decide one way or another if
she was "all in." Just like Anders hugging the saguaro.

The plank was still across the rift. Her neighbors
lined up quietly and filed across it to the other side.
Some of them looked back and waved, but most of them
just began running.

Joanna was the last one.

She embraced Maggie.

"You should come now," Joanna said. "They're going to find out sooner rather than later that people are
escaping."

"I know," Maggie said. "But I'm not ready."

"Jack," Joanna said. "Tell her to come with me. You,
too."

Jack laughed. "You think I have any influence with
her? I don't think so. And I've got one more group to
take."

"Okay," Joanna said. "I'll see you soon, partner."

Maggie nodded. Her throat tightened.

"I'll see you soon," she said.

Joanna crossed the plank and disappeared into the
desert brush.

Jack and Maggie walked back to Maggie's place. They sat on the bunkhouse porch listening to the desert stillness.

"I can hardly believe it has worked so well," Maggie said. "I figured they would come down on us a lot quicker."

Jack nodded. "Sometimes I think they count on that. They're not as competent as we think they are."

"Whoever 'they' are," Maggie said. "Where is Anders? I don't want to leave without seeing him."

"Don't worry about him," Jack said. "I bet he's right here someplace watching."

The evening drone flew overhead.

Neighbors began gathering for the last trip across.

Anders didn't show up.

Neither did Lisa and Ricardo. Probably because no one had told them. No one trusted them enough to tell them.

At least *Maggie* didn't trust them. She suspected they had told Shaw about Anders and that was why the storm troopers had broken into her house.

But what if they hadn't done anything?

Was she really going to let them stay here while Shaw and his men built a wall or gassed the neighborhood?

"Jack," Maggie said. "Wait for me. I won't be long."

Maggie got on her bike and rode to Ricardo's house. She hesitated before getting off her bike. If they were in league with Shaw and she told them about the escape plan, she and Jack and the rest of the neighbors would never get away.

She got off the bike and went to the door. She knocked.

And knocked.

Ricardo opened the door.

"Margarita, come in, come in," he said. "We've been so worried."

"Listen," Maggie said. "I'm not coming in. I wanted to tell you that Jeff Shaw told me they are going to gas us all tomorrow—or the next day. Some kind of sleeping gas they claim. And they're going to build a wall to keep us all in here."

"That is nonsense," he said. "They would never do that to us. We are citizens of this country!"

"It's been nearly two weeks since the rift appeared," Maggie said. "They aren't fixing it. Things are getting worse. If you and your family want to get to the other side, I can help you, but you have to leave now."

"What are you saying?"

"We made a bridge," Maggie said. "If you want to go across the rift, I can take you now. You can pack a bag and bring some water. But it's now or never. And bring flashlights if you're coming."

Ricardo left the door open as he went into the house. Maggie could hear him talking to Lisa in the kitchen. She heard Alicia's voice, too. She couldn't understand the words.

She looked around as she waited.

A few minutes later, Ricardo was at the door. He came out, carrying a backpack. Alicia and Lisa followed him. Alicia said hello. Lisa didn't say a word.

"Better let the horses go or make certain they can get to the hay," Maggie said.

Alicia dropped her pack and ran to the barn.

The three adults stood waiting, silently.

When Alicia returned, Maggie got back on her bike.

"I'll meet you at the house."

It was nearly dark by the time Ricardo and his family reached Maggie's house. They joined the rest of their neighbors. Then Jack took them onto the path to the rift.

No one said anything for a long while.

Then Alicia said, "The solar eclipse begins pretty soon. We won't be able to see it, though."

"I thought the eclipse was tomorrow," Maggie said.

"Nope, today, or tonight," Alicia said. "They'll see it in Australia."

Coyotes began howling near by.

The sky turned red near the horizon. Pink spread up to the clouds overhead.

Then it was dark and they were at the rift. Maggie could barely see it in the dark. Wasn't certain how they had even made it here through the cacti and mesquite. And now they were standing on the edge of the rift.

Jack flashed the light on it. The plank looked perilously narrow.

"We're supposed to walk across that?" Lisa asked.

"It's that or walk on back," Jack said.

Ricardo stepped to the edge. Then he put his foot on the wood. He quickly walked across.

"No *problemo,*" he said. "Come on."

Alicia went next. Then Lisa.

They disappeared into the darkness without a backward glance.

Then the others crossed. Quietly. Silently.

Until only Jack and Maggie remained.

"You go now, Jack," Maggie said. "I want to find Anders before I go across."

"No way," Jack said. "We're going together or not at all."

Maggie laughed. "It's not like we're in this together."

"Yes, we are."

"Shhh," Maggie said.

She heard footsteps on the other side of the rift. Saw lights flashing as though someone was walking with a helmet light and a flashlight.

A whole line of someones.

Jack leaned over and reached for the plank, to pull it away. Maggie leaned over, too. The two of them pulled on it. The far end fell off the rift. They couldn't hold onto it, so they let it drop. It fell soundlessly into the abyss.

Jack and Maggie turned and began running down the path, a dangerous thing to do in the desert at night. When they were certain they were well out of sight of the rift, they slowed. Jack started to turn on his flashlight, but Maggie stopped him.

"You don't need it," she said. "Look, we can see."

The plants were lighting the way for them. Maggie glanced behind her. No light there.

They hurried across Fifth Street and dropped down into the wash.

Everything felt different.

This is the time and place where all wounds are healed.

The wash shimmered. The sand was glowing.

Or it wasn't.

Something was racing toward them. It stopped in front of them, a towering mountain of horse.

The blue-black horse.

He had on a bridle. No bit.

Maggie went up to his face. He nuzzled her. She kissed his forehead. Then she went to his left side.

Jack interlaced his fingers to give Maggie a boost up. She was soon up and over the horse.

"Now you," she said.

He laughed. "I don't think it's possible."

She held her hand out to him. "I am an Amazon." Jack took her hand. She pulled him up and over the horse.

He slipped up against her.

"Sorry," he said. "It's the way the horse slopes."

Maggie laughed. The horse moved slowly forward. She leaned back against Jack. He put his arms around her waist. She closed her eyes. How comfortable this was.

When she opened her eyes, she saw a light in the wash. They were near the fence Gabriel had put up, only the fence was no longer there.

Anders was standing in the middle of the wash. He looked as he had that first night: his skin almost translucent, his body a light. Jack got off the horse. Maggie came down next.

She walked over to Anders, slip-sliding on the sand a bit.

He put his arms around her, and they embraced.

"It is time," he said.

Maggie nodded.

"You are the best companion I ever had," he said. "I am grateful that you called me here."

"I called you?" she asked.

"Either you or Coyote Jack did," he said. "Or maybe it was all an accident, a rip in the fabric between worlds. Or maybe I'm an alien. Or a terrorist. Or it's all a dream."

Maggie laughed. "Stop! You're making me dizzy."

Anders smiled.

"This has been the strangest two weeks of my life," Maggie said.

"It's not over," Anders said. He kissed Maggie on the lips. For an instant, she felt regret. Maybe she should have, could have, would have.

Then Anders embraced Jack. He kissed him on the mouth, too.

"Have a good life," Anders said.

They were surrounded by jackrabbits. Maggie wondered how long they had been there.

The light in the wash got bigger. The ground beneath her seemed to shift a bit. Anders and the horse walked around a corner in the wash and disappeared from sight.

The light went out.

Maggie took Jack's hand.

"I wish he could have stayed forever," she said.

"Me, too."

NEXT TO THE LAST

Maggie barely remembered going into her house or falling to sleep. She had the sense throughout the night that someone was with her. Jack? But she was too sleepy to come fully awake.

When she opened her eyes to morning, she wondered if it had all been a dream.

She was tempted to run down the road to see if the rift was gone.

Instead she got dressed and went outside with her rattle. She went to the bunkhouse and knocked on the door. No one answered. She walked over to the garden. Jack was inside, tending to the plants. The whole garden had grown up in a way no garden could grow in two weeks. It was green and juicy looking. Jack looked so tender as he leaned over the plants, his lips moving, his hands reaching out to touch the leaves. A plant whisperer, Coyote Jack. Who would have guessed?

Maggie walked back to the middle of the driveway. She began to rattle and sing.

"Up, Sun, up! We love and need you! Up, Sun, up! We sing to you in deep love and gratitude! Up, Sun, up!" She did a little dance in the sand.

"Up, Sun, up!" Maggie heard Jack's voice behind her. She turned around. Jack stood in the sun, dressed in blue jeans and a blue denim shirt. He smiled and wrinkles grew around his blue eyes.

She walked up to him, took his face between her hands, and kissed him on the lips. Then she said, "I want to trip the light fantastic with you."

He smiled. "All right then."

"It was you all along, wasn't it?" Maggie asked. "Making the garden grow. You're the magic man. The magic coyote."

Jack put his arm around her waist. "I ain't no coyote, Mags," he said. "I'm just a man. Whether I'm magic or not, that is to be determined. I was a botanist in another life and then a gardener."

Maggie nodded. "I don't want to stay here and be fenced in or gassed or whatever they're going to do. And I don't want to cross the rift to the other side. I don't want that life. You got any ideas?"

"Maybe the rift is mended," he said. "You could stay here and keeping doing what you've been doing."

"It'll never be the same. And I can't keep trying to mend the world one person at a time."

"Is that what you've been doing?" Jack asked. He shook his head. "Maybe the world doesn't need mending. Maybe it's just the people who need fixing."

Maggie shook her head. "If I stay here, I'm afraid I'll just be afraid. I want something else. I want a life of

   KIM ANTIEAU

magic and adventure. I want a life of routine and change and wonder. Whatever life I have, I want to be all in. You know? I don't want to be on the edge of anything."

"Well, Mags," Jack said, looking toward the Rincon Mountains. "There's always the mountains. I've long wanted to see what's on the other side. Maybe Boxer and Crazy Lu will consent to carry us over."

"I like that idea," Maggie said. She grinned. "But first we have some other business to attend to."

She took Jack's hand and led him toward the house.

"Aren't we running for our lives?" he asked.

"This shouldn't take long," she said.

"Yep. I knew you were the one I've been looking for."

ABOUT THE AUTHOR

Kim Antieau has written many novels, short stories, poems, and essays. Her work has appeared in numerous publications, both in print and online, including *The Magazine of Fantasy and Science Fiction, Asimov's SF, The Clinton Street Quarterly, The Journal of Mythic Arts, EarthFirst!, Alternet, Sage Woman,* and *Alfred Hitchcock's Mystery Magazine.* She was the founder, editor, and publisher of *Daughters of Nyx: A Magazine of Goddess Stories, Mythmaking, and Fairy Tales.* Her work has twice been short-listed for the Tiptree Award, and has appeared in many Best of the Year anthologies. Critics have admired her "literary fearlessness" and her vivid language and imagination. Her first novel *The Jigsaw Woman* is a modern classic of feminist literature. She has also written *The Gaia Websters, Butch, Her Frozen Wild, The Fish Wife,* and *Church of the Old Mermaids.* Kim lives in the Pacific Northwest with her husband, writer Mario Milosevic. Learn more about Kim and her writing at www.kimantieau.com.